THE QUEEN OF NIGHTMARES

USA TODAY BESTSELLING AUTHOR

R SULLINS

The Queen of Nightmares

THE NIGHTMARE DUET

R SULLINS

www.rsullins.com

rsullinsauthor@gmail.com

Cover by RJ Creatives

For my NBC girls, you know who you are! Long live the King!

Foreword

I will never do justice to this story, I already know that, and it wasn't my goal. My only goal was to create something entertaining, something you can get lost in and take your mind off the reality of the world we live in.

Jack is one of my favorite characters. He is so nuanced, with so many layers to him. He feels the weight of the responsibility which he readily accepts, but he also feels the pull toward something… *more.*

I hope I managed to do this incredible character justice as I created a world for him in which he ruled a slightly different Halloween town.

Welcome to Pumpkin Patch, Utah.

THE QUEEN OF NIGHTMARES

I rolled over, stretching out my arm, reaching for something that I instinctively knew wouldn't be there. Every day for the past two months has been the same. Ever since I left the hospital with the thick bandage on my forearm where the doctor had attempted to dismember it from my body, I have woken up alone. I knew Jack wasn't far away, and I also knew he slept beside me, the indentation in his pillow where his head lay the night before. I could also swear I could still feel the sensation of his arms holding me as I slept. Though, that was likely nothing more than wishful thinking on my part.

The moment I woke up in the hospital, confusion and pain over-whelmed me. I had searched the room with blurry vision, trying to blink back the mental fog as I searched the room, expecting to find Jack. Instead, I saw Kara sitting in a chair in the corner, typing away on her phone. I stared at her for several seconds, trying to come to terms with the fact that it was a casually dressed Kara wearing jeans and a T-shirt with me and not the man that I loved.

The door opened abruptly, and a nurse came into the room. Kara looked up from her phone for just a second, then returned to her screen before her head jerked back up.

"Oh my god, you're awake!" She quickly jumped out of her chair and rushed to my bedside. "Holy shit, girl. Everyone has been so worried about you!"

"Jack…" my voice was nothing but a harsh croak, making me realize how dry and raw my throat felt. I tried to lift my arm to rub at the soreness there when agonizing pain flooded through every part of me, starting at my arm.

The nurse tutted, then hit a button lying next to me on the bed.

"This is your morphine, sweetie. You press that whenever you feel you need to. It's a much lower dose than normal, considering the pregnancy, but it should help take the edge off. If you hit your limit and you're still in pain, you press that call button and let me know."

Immediately, a weightless feeling began to flood me, and I could feel my eyelids begin to droop. "Jack?"

"Sweetie, that man hasn't left your side since you were admitted here two days ago." The nurse smiled down at me with a dreamy look that told me what she thought of my luck at having Jack at my bedside. "He had to leave, but I'm sure he'll be back as soon as he can."

Kara rubbed my knee through the hospital blanket. "Sorry, I'm not who you want to see right now, but all the club members are at Lock's funeral. I'm sure Bones will be back later tonight if he can make it. Though, I heard they are having a huge party in Lock's honor instead of a wake. Bones will probably want to stay for that since Lock was his VP and all."

I stopped listening as memories of seeing Lock standing in front of me, his red shirt turning wet as blood seeped into it. I remembered seeing his lips move as if he were trying to speak. The memories morphed from watching Lock fall face forward toward me to the sight of Zero lying motionless in the dirt. I wanted to scream out at the agony that filled my chest, but all I could do was close my eyes and drift off to sleep again as a tear escaped from the corner of my eye.

That was two months ago, and though Kara was wrong and Jack had returned to my room as soon as the funeral was over instead of going to the party, his absence had remained just as vivid ever since. Despite his presence, I might as well have been alone.

Most of the time, even though Jack was near, he was distracted or on the phone speaking in a gruff, hushed tone. Pain medication made it difficult for me to understand what he was saying. Since we came home and I started getting better, he took his calls in another room. I understood that it was important club business. I couldn't imagine what he was going through. I just wished he would look at me for more than the few seconds he'd glance my way before his eyes turned hard as ice and his jaw clenched as he ground his molars. Whenever he'd jerk his gaze away from me again, my heart clenched a little bit harder. I didn't blame him, though. I hated me, too. Lock would still be alive if it weren't for me.

I gingerly sat up, hoping that it would be the morning I wouldn't have to run for the toilet, but the moment I was fully upright, sitting on the edge of the mattress, my stomach rebelled. I quickly scrambled around the end of the bed, nearly hitting my shin on the bedframe as I slid along the floor in my haste and made it to the toilet just in time to kneel carefully on the tile floor before losing the meager contents of my stomach.

When I was done, I flushed the toilet and waited patiently, breathing deeply through my nose while wiping my eyes and nose with toilet tissue. Sometimes, the nausea would linger, forcing me to drop right back down to the floor to heave a few more times. Fortunately, it seemed like it would be a good morning. As I let out a long exhale, the nausea seemed to stay at a manageable level.

I finally got up, rising just a little unsteadily to my feet. I crossed over to the sink, quickly brushing my teeth before heading back to the toilet to pee. I may have been squeezing my legs together there towards the end when I was spitting the toothpaste suds out into the sink, but getting the awful taste of vomit out of my mouth took priority over relieving my bladder.

I glanced at the shower, wanting to get cleaned up, but my energy levels were at rock bottom, and I just couldn't bring myself to care. I turned back to the bedroom, walking around the foot of the bed to my side much slower that time, as Zero sat there, thumping his tail on the floor as he stared up at me with his wide doggy eyes. I sat down on the mattress with a heavy sigh as I eyed the hot mint tea and ginger cookies on my nightstand. Jack may have been more like a ghost around the house since I came home from the hospital, but he was still taking care of me. I blinked back the tears that threatened and rubbed a finger under my suddenly stinging nose, refusing to cry. Zero jumped onto the bed beside me and shoved his wet nose against my leg with a low whine. I absently stroked his scruff as I stared down into the steam curling from the tea.

I hadn't allowed myself to cry since the first couple of weeks that we'd returned home after my release from the hospital. Jack's physical presence but mental and emotional separation from me hurt so keenly. It was as if I could literally feel my heart cracking into pieces in my chest with every beat. I used to lock myself in the bathroom and cry tears as silently as I could. But after I overheard Jack talking to someone on the phone about having difficulty replacing Lock as Vice President, I stopped letting the tears fall. I didn't deserve to let them. But I could do nothing about the ache in my chest.

I reached for the teacup with my left hand. As I wrapped my fingers around the handle, they were already beginning to tremble. I lifted the cup slowly, raising it two inches, then three off the wooden surface of the nightstand before the muscles in my arm started shaking so badly with the strain that a bit of the liquid sloshed over the side of the cup. I couldn't hold the weight any longer and had to use my right hand to support the steaming tea before I dropped it and made another mess like the one I had made a few days ago in the kitchen.

With the help of my right hand, I brought the cup to my lips, lightly blowing on it before taking a sip. Jack made it perfectly, exactly how I liked it, with just a bit of honey. I didn't know how a man who couldn't stand the sight of me still cared enough to ensure my needs were being met. I closed my eyes as a new wave of pain swept through me. Perhaps it wasn't me that he was caring for now. I was pregnant with his child. A part of me that got louder every day couldn't help but wonder if I would still be sitting here in his home if I had lost the baby.

I shook my head as my nose stung and my eyes filled with tears again. But I looked up at the ceiling and blinked them back before any could fall. I wouldn't allow myself to feel sorry for this situation I had found myself in. I thought of Lock and how he would smile as if he were always looking around the world and seeing how we were all fools. He was loyal and had a good heart. He had been the one responsible for Jack coming to my rescue the first night they had returned from the rally. If it wasn't for Lock, I might have ended up the victim of sexual assault.

With a shaky arm, I slowly lowered the teacup to the nightstand. As the hot liquid sloshed over onto my fingers, I hissed in pain. Before I knew what was happening, Jack was stomping through the bedroom and into the bathroom. I could hear the water turn on for a brief moment before turning off again, and then he was in front of me. His large tattooed fingers engulfed my hand as he pressed the cool washcloth to the slight burn.

With a quick glance at my face before putting all his concentration on the cloth in his hand, he rumbled out an admonishment that made me feel two inches tall. "You need to watch what you're doing."

I swallowed through the lump in my throat and nodded weakly as I stared at his fingers, holding the cloth in place. I couldn't speak. I knew he was right, but I could feel the irritation coming off of him in waves as he held my hand in his. In all the time we had been together, even at the beginning, I couldn't remember feeling this way with him, and it hurt so badly.

Through my lashes, I could see him glance back up at me with a frown. Without another word, he straightened to his full height from where he'd been leaning over me. I could no longer see any part of him other than the bottoms of his legs and feet. He was already wearing his heavy motorcycle boots, and I knew he was about to leave for the clubhouse. He never stayed around the house for long anymore, and he hadn't asked me to go with him to sit in his office while he worked since before the *incident*.

He paused for a long moment before turning and walking away. His footsteps stopped at the doorway, and I heard him tap his knuckles against the wooden door frame.

"I'll bring something back for dinner." A long pause. "Make sure you take your pill and stretch your arm." Then he was striding down the hall, his heavy footsteps fading away. There was a pause, and then the front door opened, and I could hear the double beep of the alarm followed by a series of beeps as he armed it.

I glanced at the pill bottle on my nightstand next to the ginger cookies, the prenatal vitamins staring at me. Jack wanted me to take them, reminded me daily, and those were often the only words he spoke to me. A part of me wanted to throw the bottle across the room. I sighed and reached for the vitamins with my left hand since I wouldn't have a strong enough grip to twist the lid off unless I used my right hand. I opened the bottle and then fished out one of the large pills. With a grimace, I placed it on my tongue and then picked up the fresh water bottle that was magically always there for me. I washed down the pill with several gulps of the cool water, then ate a cookie before my stomach could make too much of a fuss.

With a sigh, I settled back against my pillow and reclined on the bed, thinking about the long, boring day ahead. I didn't know if Kara would visit me today. She was the only one I ever saw aside from Jack. The few short times I saw him each day should have made me happy. Instead, every time he left, it just widened the hole in my heart a little more. My chest was always aching these days. I had thought that nothing could hurt as badly as my arm when I first woke up in the hospital. I was wrong.

CHAPTER
Two

THE QUEEN OF NIGHTMARES

I was washing the teacup and small plate in the kitchen sink when I heard the doorbell ringing from the front door. I quickly dried my hands with a kitchen towel and all but ran to let Kara in. I needed the company, or I was going to go out of my mind.

I peeked through the peephole to be safe, then grinned when I saw Kara holding up a bag that was clearly from the deli in town.

I swung the door open wide to let the gorgeous blonde enter. Immediately, the alarm started shrieking its ear-splitting scream. "Shit! Shit! Shit! I forgot to turn off the alarm! One second," I yelled as I frantically punched in the code to disarm the alarm, then let out a breath at the sudden silence. "Damn, Jack's going to be pissed," I whispered. I shut the door, punched the code back in to reset the alarm, and turned to see Kara watching me with shrewd eyes.

I pasted on a bright smile, trying to pretend that my chest wasn't heaving from the stressful moment. "Hey! I'm so glad you're here."

She returned my smile with one that looked almost as forced as mine was. "Hey, girl. Are you okay? Is Bones going to do anything to you for setting the alarm off?"

I waved away her concern. No, I didn't think Jack would hurt me. I just hated seeing the disappointment or the frustration that he always seemed to look at me with these days. I longed to see him smile at me the way he used to, and setting off the alarm wasn't going to give him a reason to be happy. "No, of course not. I just know he will be concerned after what happened before, you know?"

I led her into the living room and gestured for her to take a seat on the leather sectional. "I'll go grab a couple of plates. Do you want a soda?"

Kara nodded as she sat down on one end of the couch, and I went into the kitchen. My phone was still on the counter where I left it, and I could see it was lighting up with a phone call from Jack already. The alarm company had likely called him the second the door opened. I let out a gust of breath, then picked it up, knowing I had probably already missed at least one call from him. If I didn't answer this time, I would bet every earthly possession I owned that he would send the entire club out here, guns blazing.

"Hey, Jack," I said quietly.

"Is everything okay? Do I need to come back to the house?" His voice was gravelly and rushed, the concern just barely discernable under the harsh tone.

"No, everything is alright. I forgot to turn the alarm off before I opened the door." I walked to the fridge and pulled on the door, having to give it a little extra effort with my left hand. "I'm sorry for worrying you."

There was a deep sigh from the phone as I grabbed two cans of soda from the fridge. "Damn it, Sally. You have to be more careful."

I swallowed back the retort that wanted to come to the surface. I wished I could say what I really wanted to. It was on the tip of my tongue to ask Jack if it was me he cared about or his baby, but I clamped my teeth shut. It wasn't until I heard nothing but silence that I blinked and pulled the cell phone away from my ear to look at the black screen. He hung up just like that, without a single word of goodbye.

I clenched my jaw and closed my eyes for a minute. *Damn it, Jack.* I couldn't keep doing this. Not for the next six months. Not for the next eighteen years. I loved that man more than life itself. But I couldn't, just couldn't keep going the way we were. I needed him to be my Jack again. I needed him to hold me and tell me everything was okay between us.

I picked up the plates and sodas when I heard Kara call out to me. When I walked back into the living room, she looked at me with concern. "Are you okay, Sally?"

I gave a small laugh that sounded as far from cheerful as I felt. I placed the plates down on the coffee table where the sandwiches had been set out. Kara had opened the wrappers on the subs and had two bags of chips sitting there waiting.

"Yeah, I'm okay. Jack was just worried, that's all."

She eyed me dubiously but picked up her sub sandwich, transferred it to her plate, and wadded up the paper it had been wrapped in. "You can talk to me, you know."

I sat down with a huff, then picked up the remote. I didn't want to talk about my issues with Jack. It felt like a betrayal to even have her asking. But I did appreciate that she worried about me.

"I know, Kara. I really appreciate it. But there isn't anything to worry about. I promise." I pushed the button to turn on the TV, ignoring her skeptical stare at the side of my face. "Which episode were we on?"

I flipped through the apps until I found the right one, quickly finding our show and starting it where we had left off before she could say anything else. She grunted from beside me and then took a huge bite of her food. I chose to ignore everything: the pain in my heart, the worry about the weakness in my still healing arm, and the baby that was my only tether to the man I would never stop loving. I picked up my sandwich and my plate, then settled back to get lost in the problems of the make-believe world on the TV.

"I think you should come to the party tonight."

Kara's words jarred me from the story playing out in front of me, and I turned to look at her, popping the last chip from the bag into my mouth. "What party?" I asked, covering my mouth as I chewed with one hand to ask her the question.

"You didn't know? There's a huge club party tonight. You've already missed the other ones. I think you should come out to the one tonight." She tipped back her head, finishing the last of her soda before leaning forward to set the empty can beside her plate. "People are starting to talk."

"Talk about what, exactly?" I turned to face her on the couch, the show forgotten.

She eyed me incredulously. "About what? Girl, no one has seen you since before the whole kidnap and murder thing. Bones is always at the club. People think you two aren't even together anymore."

Her words hurt, even if they were all true. "What does it matter if they see me?"

Her mouth dropped open for a long minute, then snapped shut. "Let me put it bluntly. Bones is a hot as fuck guy. He's powerful and important to the club and the town. There's not a single club girl that wouldn't give her right arm to have that man."

She winced as she seemed to realize what words just came out of her mouth. I looked down at my left arm. There was a long, bright pink line that was healed, but barely. The scar looked a million times better than the ones running next to it, but since it was so new, it looked awful. Dr. Stein had managed to cut pretty deep before he'd been stopped when Jack broke into the hotel room. He hadn't gotten a chance to begin sawing through my bone, but the damage he'd done to the muscle was making it hard for me to gain strength back.

"I'm really sorry, sweetie. That was insensitive of me. I wasn't thinking."

I waved away her concern, knowing she hadn't meant it. It was honestly a little funny when I thought about the stupid phrase. People didn't think about things when they said them. I knew I had said the same thing in the past when it came to ridiculous things that ultimately didn't even matter.

"Forget it. No big deal." I tilted my head and studied her. "There's not a single girl who doesn't want him, huh?"

"Girl, no! Anyone would want to be in your shoes. And since everyone now knows that he's actually into women, they all want him to choose them next."

"Even you?" I asked quietly.

She froze while reaching into her small bag of chips and looked at me with big blue eyes. Kara was gorgeous with her big breasts and perfect hourglass figure. She had big, plump lips and honey-blonde hair that she liked to play with, always running her fingers through it and adjusting the strands to curve around her breasts, accentuating them. She was also kind. She was the first nice person I had worked with at the bar, not treating me like I had a disease just because I was covered in scars. Jack could do worse. Any man would want Kara.

She choked out her words. "Me? What? No, I would never do that to you. I swear!" But I could see in her eyes the lie there. Jack was too much of a man to turn down. He was everything she had described and more. If he crooked his finger at her, she would go willingly, friendship be damned.

I gave her a small smile even as my gut twisted. "Okay, Kara. Tell me about this party."

She seemed to relax at the change of subject. "It's just the usual club party. There will be lots of music, lots of booze. Some girls will dance on the stage to the heavy rock music that always plays. It gets pretty wild. It usually doesn't take long for clothes to come off. People will start fucking on the pool tables while everyone watches or finds their own partner to fuck."

I cleared my throat and shifted uncomfortably in my seat. It wasn't something I was interested in seeing. That first night, when the whole club had shown up at the bar, and I had met Jack for the first time, was wild and crazy. I couldn't imagine sitting there watching something even more wild than that night had been.

"What does Jack usually do during these parties?" There was no way he participated. He hadn't touched a woman before me.

Kara scoffed. "That man just sits in the corner with a beer and watches. Nothing gets to him. He doesn't even allow the girls to try to get close." It was a relief to hear, even if I'd already known. Kara's tone was hesitant when she added, "But, girl, that's going to change now. You know that, right?"

I jerked my eyes back to her from where I was glancing at the TV, absently wondering what I had missed in the show. "What do you mean?"

"Once a man has had a pussy on his dick, do you *really* think that he's going to keep sitting back watching everyone else get off? Fuck no! He's going to want pussy, and there are plenty of girls just waiting for the first indication that he's ready."

I leaned back in my seat and stared at the TV, no longer seeing the show. Instead, all I could picture was a horny Jack seeing all the sex going on around him, deciding that he was bored and wanted a piece of the action. *Over my dead and dismembered body.*

CHAPTER
Three

THE QUEEN OF NIGHTMARES

Kara helped me get ready after laughing at what I had walked into the living room wearing, telling me that I wasn't heading to church. Instead of dressing in the cute sundress with a cardigan to ward off the cold weather, I was sporting a pair of the short shorts Jack had bought me months ago. It paired nicely with a lacy tank top that showed a bit of the enhanced cleavage I'd gained thanks to my pregnancy. I had to struggle just a bit with the button on the shorts. My belly wasn't showing yet. I didn't even have the slightest bump, but my lower abdomen was firmer to the touch than it used to be. The baby was clearly growing, and I had no doubts that the bump I had been looking for in the last few days would be making its appearance soon.

I sat on the bathroom counter as Kara put the finishing touches on my makeup. I was afraid to look in the mirror. I didn't even own half of what she had applied to my face. She'd gone out to her car and returned with a makeup bag that was bulging on the sides with products. When she'd held up black eyeshadow and told me I'd look great with smokey eyes, I'd just sighed in defeat and let her do whatever she wanted.

Eventually, Kara stepped back, screwing closed the lid on the stain she'd just finished applying to my lips. "There! All done! The guys are going to be creaming in their pants when they get a look at you!" I cringed at the visual but hopped down carefully from my perch on the counter.

I turned slowly to face the mirror, not expecting to look like a clown but still worried about what I'd see. My face felt almost heavy with all the products that I was wearing. When I was trying to hide my scars, I used a pretty thick concealer and foundation, but since I started wearing makeup in high school, I have generally only worn some mascara and lipgloss.

My mouth dropped open in shock when I looked at my reflection. The scars on my face were barely discernible, but that wasn't what had surprised me. The dark eye makeup paired with the bright red lip stain made my blue eyes pop. The contouring she had done made my cheekbones look camera-ready. I almost looked like a model. I didn't know if I loved it or hated it. But there was no doubt I looked good, even if I barely resembled myself.

"Wow," I breathed as I turned my face from one side to the other, looking for the tell-tell signs of the scars that ran from the corners of my lip to nearly my ears, giving me the hideous smile I hated but had grown used to seeing whenever I looked in a mirror. She had done a fantastic job. "I might need some pointers for the future."

"I got you, girl. Any time, really." Kara quickly added some eyeshadow to her own lids as I watched and gave her eyes an exotic look with some liquid eyeliner that extended out past the corners of her eyes. I turned to look at the corners of my own eyes to see she had done the same to mine, though not quite as dramatically as she had with hers.

I heard her zip up her makeup bag and looked back to see she had already put on some lip stain. Her look was flawless, and I could imagine her easily making a killing as an influencer on social media.

She looked me up and down. "Ready to go wow the club?"

Nope. "Uh, yeah. I guess."

"That's the spirit!"

She giggled as she hooked her arm with mine and led me into the bedroom. I picked up the cardigan against her protests and shrugged it on. It was really freaking cold. No matter what she said, I wasn't going outside in just a tank top.

When we reached the door, I bit my lip before remembering the lip stain. Kara had promised it would last the whole night and that I would be able to eat and drink without having to stress about smudges or fading, but I couldn't help but be worried. I stared at the alarm panel a sucked in a huge breath. I hadn't been outside since the hospital except for brief trips to the doctor to have my stitches removed weeks ago and to check on my healing progress shortly after that. I was due for an appointment with my obstetrician in a couple of days, but this would be the first time I left without Jack by my side.

I let the breath out slowly, then punched in the code. There was a possibility that Jack would just think I was letting Kara out or she was retrieving something from the car like earlier. However, if he decided to look at the app on his phone, he would see that I set the alarm to AWAY instead of the STAY setting, indicating I was leaving. I shrugged one shoulder defiantly. Oh well. I wasn't his prisoner. I could leave any time I wanted to. Right. *Shit.*

My fingers trembled as I stepped out the door, followed by Kara, and fit the key into the lock. I wasn't so sure about this plan anymore. I didn't really mind staying inside the house where it was safe. I slipped the key into the back pocket of my shorts and lifted my chin defiantly. I couldn't live like a princess locked away in a tower. Maybe Jack would be mad; he would just have to get over it.

I followed Kara to her beat-up little car. It looked like it had been through a few battles and lost. I eyed it dubiously as she climbed inside the driver's seat. She leaned over and unlocked the passenger door for me. It gave a loud metallic groan as I pulled it open, and I gingerly sat down on the stained cloth seat. It was clean inside but obviously worn down with age.

The car started up with a little grumbling, like a kid who didn't want to wake up for school, but once she put it into drive, it rode smoothly. Kara ran her hand over the cracked dash and grinned at me.

"My brother is a mechanic. Someone brought this little guy in but couldn't pay the bill. Since the garage keeps the cars from people who don't pay their bills, he fixed it up and gave it to me as a birthday gift a couple of years ago. It runs great, and he keeps up on the maintenance for free."

"Oh, that was nice of him. Who's your brother?"

She waved her hand as we approached the clubhouse. The heavy metal door was propped open, and light spilled into the parking lot that was filled with almost as many cars as there were bikes. "You don't know him. He doesn't live in Pumpkin Patch."

I was going to ask more questions, but the words died on my tongue as I got my first view of the new gate. It was a massive black wrought iron with wide brick posts on either side. There was a guy standing at the gate looking bored and wearing a leather vest. As he turned away, I could see his cut didn't have a patch on the back. I realized he was a prospect likely on gate duty for the night.

I turned and saw the wrought iron fencing stretched on as far as I could see, going toward Jack's place. Turning my head, I could see it stretching in the opposite direction as well. Jack had fenced in the Devil's Nightmares compound. My heart did a funny flip in my chest. I hadn't known he'd installed the fence. It hadn't been there the last time I came through, but that had been at least a few weeks ago. I never noticed a fence outside the house, but then I rarely looked outside. It also was possible the fence wasn't very close to the house, either. But one thing was certain: Jack wanted the compound safe from intruders like Dr. Stein.

I blew out a breath and looked over to Kara, who had walked to my side. "There's a fence."

She giggled and hooked her arm with mine, leading me toward the front door that was propped open, loud music blaring from inside. "Yeah. It has been all the town has been talking about for weeks." She bumped her hip into mine. "Ready to turn some heads?"

"Not even a little bit," I muttered under my breath as I took the first step inside the spacious room.

I had seen it before when I used to come with Jack to his office, but it had never looked the way it did now. The lights were on, but they were turned down low enough to give off the atmosphere of a club. An actual dance club, not a motorcycle club.

The small stage in the corner that had a pole on it was occupied by two girls writhing against each other, wearing next to nothing. A handful of bikers holding beer bottles shouted encouragement to the girls as they caressed each other while sliding around the pole. They weren't dancing or using the pole as intended. It was more like a prop as they got the men worked up into a frenzy.

The two pool tables in the middle of the room had several bikers surrounding them. A couple of the men were holding pool sticks, attempting to play an actual game, while the other guys were making out with or groping more scantily clad women. I watched as a biker picked up one girl by her butt and sat her heavily down on the table. He ripped her leather bikini top down over her breasts, laughing as they popped out, baring her pierced nipples.

I looked away quickly, only for my eyes to land on one of the leather couches. A girl was on her knees in front of Barrel, who had his legs spread wide, his thighs on either side of her chest as her head bobbed up and down furiously. His half-lidded eyes met mine, and I watched as his gaze slid lazily over my body. His lips turned up in a smile right before he froze, his eyes widening in shock.

I saw the second he recognized me and held back my cringe. I wanted to turn around and run back out the door before he could sound the alarm, but I squared back my shoulders. I wasn't going to run. I belonged here, didn't I? I was the President's woman. I may not have a tattoo on my wrist telling the world that I was Devil's Nightmare property, but I was owned just the same.

Barrel sat up straighter as his eyes narrowed on me while the head continued to bob quickly in his lap. I could feel his censure and knew he disapproved of me showing up here tonight. Well, fuck that. I started to turn away when I felt a heavy arm wrap around my waist and pull me into a hard, muscled body. It took me only a second to realize that the man holding me wasn't Jack.

"Hey, sweetheart. Haven't seen you around here before. Lucky me, I get to claim your hot little body before all my brothers get ahold of you. I do hate sloppy seconds." The voice was rough, slightly accented with a southern drawl, and definitely not what I wanted to hear. His hot breath fanned over my neck before I felt his wet tongue lick me there and slide up to my ear. "Oh yeah, I'm gonna have fun riding you tonight."

"Don't touch me. I belong to Jack." I tried to pull away, but he tightened his grip with a laugh.

"I don't know who Jack is, but baby, if you walk in here looking like that all alone, you're going to find out real quick that any *Jack* will do."

"I don't even know what that means!" I twisted to face the guy I had never seen before.

"It means you're fair game, baby." He grinned at me with straight white teeth. He was handsome, with dark hair and brown eyes. He had a thick beard that was nicely trimmed, but he was so, so wrong.

"The Nightmares don't take women against their will." I gritted out as I pushed against him again. "And Jack is…"

He cut me off before I could finish my sentence. "No, the Nightmares don't force girls. But then, you wouldn't come to a party here if you weren't looking for a biker to get between your thighs. So stop playing hard to get, sweetheart. If you want privacy, we can find a room to fuck in."

"Jack is Bones, you dimwitted fuckface. Now, let me *go*." I yanked hard just as the man dropped me like I was on fire. The momentum had me falling backward with a yelp. He took a step forward as if to keep me from falling, but before he could reach me, I landed against a hard chest. Strong arms wrapped around me, much like the man's had just moments before. This time was different, though. This time, the arms belonged to the only man I craved.

I immediately settled into Jack's arms, my heart sighing at the feeling I had missed for the last couple of months. Now that they were wrapped around me again, I never wanted to leave them.

All too soon, Jack's hands left my body, and I opened my mouth to protest. His big hands gripped my waist and roughly moved me to the side. As I stumbled a few feet over, I watched as he stalked forward and wrapped one of those hands around the throat of the man who had thought he had a right to fuck me.

"Tell me one good reason I shouldn't gut you right here, Joker?" Jack's tone was low and deadly as I admired his back muscles flexing under his black T-shirt.

"I didn't know she was yours, Prez. She said she belonged to Jack. I don't know, man. I've been gone for almost a year. If you got an old lady, nobody mentioned it." His voice was raspy as he croaked out the words through the tight squeeze around his throat.

I stared at those tattooed fingers that were flexing as if trying to decide whether to squeeze or let go, and I brought my fingers up to my own neck. I ghosted my fingertips over the place where Jack used to hold me so possessively but no longer did. Tears blurred my vision as I turned away, pushing past the bodies that were surrounding us.

I stumbled away from the circle of onlookers and quickened my pace until I was running down the long hallway that led away from the common room where the party was being held. I ignored all the sounds coming from dark corners and passed a couple fucking up against the wall right in the hallway without a glance.

I stopped at the door to Jack's office, expecting it to be locked, surprised that it was ajar. I pushed it open to see the lamp on at the desk and a pile of papers covering the surface. Was he in here working while the party was going on down the hall?

I wiped at my eyes and looked down at my hand to see it covered in black mascara and eyeliner. Great. Now, I was going to look ridiculous. I sniffled as I stood in the center of the room and wrapped my arms around my middle. The voice from the doorway had me freezing in place while my heart immediately started pounding out of control.

JACK

"I'm going to let you live since you had no idea who she is to me. That's on me." I tightened my grip just enough that Joker couldn't mistake my intentions. "But if you even so much as breathe the same air as her with any purpose other than to protect her, I will strip the flesh from your bones and feed it to my dog." I shoved him away from me and quickly followed after my little Queen. I didn't give a fuck what anybody thought about their President chasing after his woman.

It was as if she were my beacon of light. I needed her. The only light in my darkness was my Queen. I had spent the last two months doing everything within my power to ensure her life was as safe as possible.

I pushed the door to my office open further to reveal my girl standing in the middle of the room. She was staring at my desk with a forlorn expression. I wanted to yell at her, to punish her for leaving the house unprotected. She'd entered my clubhouse without a guard and opened herself up to the lustful gazes of every biker present. I trusted them, but she was my woman. *Mine.* And nobody had the right to look at her but me. She looked beautiful with her sexy body and blood-red hair falling down to her waist. I wanted to cut the eyes out of every man who had seen her tonight, with her wearing those little shorts that showed off her toned legs.

"What are you doing here, little Queen?" I could hear the residual anger still seeping into my tone from seeing her wrapped in another man's arms. I didn't know what might have happened if Barrel hadn't come to get me. I know I would have had to kill Joker for touching more of her than he already had.

Her swift intake of breath was the only indication that she had heard me. I watched as her shoulders curled inward and her arms tightened around her middle. I took another step forward and swung the door shut before turning the lock with a loud snick.

I slowly stepped closer, afraid I would spook her. I was close enough to feel her body heat radiating off of her. I closed my eyes and dipped my head down until my nose was just a hairsbreadth away from skimming her neck. I took in a deep inhale, bringing her scent into my lungs. She smelled of sweet oranges and vanilla, and my stomach clenched at my desperate need for her.

For months, I had denied myself the feel and taste of her body. I couldn't allow myself the comfort, not when I had to make sure that what had happened could never happen again. *If I lost her…*

I clenched my fists at my sides to keep from reaching out. I had nearly lost my little Queen all because of my arrogance. Stupid mistakes had led to her being taken from me. Because of me, one of my best friends was dead. I was lucky that Zero had made a full recovery. But had Sally been killed, I wouldn't have survived the loss.

"You shouldn't have left the house. What were you thinking, coming here alone?"

"I wasn't alone."

I raised an eyebrow at her whispered words. She had been alone with my club brother in the crowded room. I thought of how she had spent her day as I watched from the cameras. She'd spent the time with the blonde friend she usually spent time with. The blonde was the only one to ever come and go. The blonde would have been the only way Sally would have even known about the party. Why did she bring my girl only to leave her on her own?

"If you wanted to come to the clubhouse, you should have asked me so I could keep an eye on you." I tried to soften my tone, but the anger still coursed through my veins. I stepped back as Sally suddenly whirled around, her long hair brushing against the bare skin of my arms, making me bite back a groan at the contact. She looked up at me with fire in her weary eyes.

She had smeared makeup on her cheek from where she had rubbed tears away, but she had never looked more beautiful than she did as she stood in front of me with her fists clenched and blue eyes flashing.

"And you would have brought me?" She scoffed, lifting her chin in such a haughty manner that it made her appear to be the queen I knew she was.

My fingers itched to swipe away the strands of red hair that stuck to her cheek. "Perhaps," I murmured.

She threw her arms out, then let them drop back to her side. "Perhaps? Perhaps you would have spent time with me? Perhaps you would have spoken more than two words to me?"

I furrowed my brows. It was true; I hadn't spent much time with Sally since the attack. I'd had a single-minded focus to fix all the security holes in my home and compound. She also needed time to heal. I glanced down at her arm to see the bright pink line where she had nearly lost her arm due to the almost nonexistent security two months ago.

"I've been busy."

"Busy doing what, Jack? Busy with who?" There was an accusation in her tone that I didn't like.

"I've been trying to make our world a safer place. You are going to have my child soon. I won't have it come into a world that is too dangerous for it to even play outside."

Her fight seemed to leave her almost as quickly as it had come. I watched as her shoulders slumped and her hands went to her abdomen. "The baby," she whispered brokenly. "Of course, you want the baby to be safe."

I tilted my head, confused by her sadness. "The baby means the world to me, Sally." Didn't she know that I would do anything, to give anything, to make sure that the piece of her currently safe in her belly would never know a moment of pain or be frightened by the world around us?

She looked back up at me, a small, sad smile on her face that didn't reach her eyes. Her eyes held nothing but bleak misery, and the sight of it made me want to howl at the moon in frustration. "I know that, Jack." She looked away from me to stare at the darkened window across the room. "I just wish…" Her words trailed off, fading away the way her light seemed to be right before my eyes. I finally gave in to my need to touch her.

I placed a finger under her chin and forced just enough pressure there to get her to turn her face back to me. I needed to see her eyes. My heart thumped wildly in my chest at the feel of her soft flesh against mine again. For so long, all I had allowed myself was to hold her at night. I have been so afraid I would hurt her. I suppose, in a way, I was also punishing myself for my mistakes that had led to her injury.

"You wish, what, little Queen?" I coaxed as I swept my thumb over her chin, close to her plump bottom lip. I couldn't see her scars under all the makeup. It made me want to demand that she wash it all off so I could see her, the real her. She always looked beautiful, but I loved her natural beauty the most.

She blinked up at me, and a tear escaped, sliding down her cheek and making a trail through the dark smears of her makeup. She let out a stuttering breath, and her voice was so soft I had to strain to hear her in the quiet room. "I wish you still loved me, too."

Her words nearly had me doubling over from the pain they caused. It felt as if someone had taken a red-hot blade and plunged it directly into my heart. My words sounded as broken and jagged as I felt.

"You don't think I love you?"

She gave me that small smile that was nothing but misery and what I suddenly recognized as heartbreak because I felt the same emotion now, too.

"I think that I wouldn't still be in your life if I weren't carrying your baby."

I closed my eyes as I felt her words hit me like serrated knives, slicing me to the bone. I thought back to every time I left her in the morning. I always ensured she had what she needed. The tea, I knew, helped with the sickness she woke up with. I didn't dare touch her while she felt so poorly. I hadn't wanted to cause her more discomfort, so I left her with the ginger cookies that the lady at the diner had assured me would help with the nausea. I would remind her to take her prenatal vitamin since the doctor had assured me it would be good for her health.

But all along, what she needed was *me.*

I opened my eyes, blinking back moisture, to see her head bowed in defeat again. I couldn't take it anymore. I had held back because she needed to heal. I had spent all my time away to ensure her safety. Most of my days were spent on the phone or in meetings with the other MC presidents, discussing plans to stop Oogie and the Boogeymen from their imminent invasion of my territory and the specific threats he had made against my woman. The only comfort I had been able to allow myself was the intimacy of holding her in her sleep. In doing what I had, I made the woman I love lose her hope.

I moved my hand, sliding it down from her chin until it rested on her neck. I could feel the soft fluttering of her heartbeat against my fingers and relished in the feel of the proof that she was alive and in front of me. I tightened my grasp until I could feel her heart beating steady and strong. She gasped and jerked her head up, her eyes meeting mine. A small spark of life flickered there as her gaze met mine.

"The baby is my world, little Queen. It exists because it's part of you. But you? You are my very existence. Without you, there is no me." Her lips trembled as she stared into my eyes, and I watched as that little flicker of life grew brighter. "I told you before that I didn't know what love is. But, Sally, the way I feel for you? It doesn't seem strong enough, but there is no other word that could describe the yearning, the obsession, the desire I feel for only you. I'm sorry I haven't shown you. But, I vow to you, not another day will go by in our very long lives that I won't show you with everything I am. I love you, little Queen."

I counted each tear that slid down her cheeks as I spoke the words from my heart until I lost count. Each tear was another misdeed I had made against her that I would strive to make up for.

"Jack." My name trembled on her lips.

"You're mine," I swore to her as I lowered my head to press my lips to hers, groaning at the contact I had been craving for months.

"I'm yours," she promised, her soft lips moving against mine. She wrapped her arms around my shoulders, diving a hand into the hair at the back of my head. "I love you, Jack. Make me yours again," she moaned against my mouth.

"You have never stopped being mine."

CHAPTER

Five

THE QUEEN OF NIGHTMARES

It seemed as if mere seconds ticked by, and I was naked in front of a fully clothed Jack. I clawed frantically at his T-shirt, desperate to feel his skin against mine but too overwhelmed to think straight. He gently removed my fingers from the tight grasp I had on his shirt and shifted my hands to my sides. Then, he reached behind his head and pulled his shirt off the way that always had my heart beating faster and anticipation building in my core.

"You're so fucking beautiful," he breathed against my lips before reaching for my thighs. He gripped them firmly and lifted me while turning and taking a few long strides to the nearest wall. With his gaze trapping me in their bottomless black depths, he pressed my back against the wall, the cool surface making me hiss and arch my breasts into his smooth, muscled chest. "You will never doubt me again." He reached between us to pull at his belt and the button of his jeans. His growled words went straight to my clit, making me shudder, while at the same time, a small pang of regret twisted my heart.

"I'm sorry," I whispered, meaning it down to my soul. I should have trusted him. I should have known that the man I knew he was would never turn his back on me so easily. After giving me everything and knowing he had trouble expressing himself, I should have given him the benefit of the doubt. My stupid emotions had been all over the place after I had woken up in the hospital. Guilt, pain, sadness, it all tormented me into thinking I was unloveable, that I didn't deserve to be loved. So why wouldn't he turn away from me? It was nothing but lies and self-doubt.

"I'm sorry I didn't give you the reassurance you needed." His expression was so tortured that I raised my hands to cup his cheeks.

"We'll know to never do this to each other again," I whispered.

"Never," he agreed roughly.

With that vow, he shifted until his hard cock was at my entrance, then he slowly pressed forward, sliding into me inch by glorious inch. The burning stretch I felt as he filled me so completely made me gasp with the pleasure I had been missing. He took advantage of my open mouth, pressing his lips to mine and plunging his tongue inside. The kiss was so sweet as his lips caressed mine that my eyes teared up with an overflow of emotions.

Once he was at the point where he could sink no deeper, he paused, allowing me to adjust to being so full again. I watched in rapt fascination as he closed his eyes, the tendons on the side of his neck straining as he groaned with pleasure. Seeing this ruthless, hard man being so overwhelmed by the feel of me was such a beautiful sight. It made me wish I could take a picture to carry with me always.

"You feel so fucking good," he growled as he opened those intense eyes again to stare at me. He withdrew as slowly as he had entered me, his long length dragging against all the sensitive nerve endings in my channel. "My pussy." He slammed his cock back into me, making me cry out from the pleasure-pain. "My woman." He pulled back only to slam back in again just as hard. "My Queen," He growled as he began to piston his hips at a brutal pace that left me whimpering as I clawed at his shoulders.

I could feel everything inside me tightening as an orgasm so huge it almost terrified me began to build. My skin was so sensitive that goosebumps covered my arms and neck, and even my scalp tingled as my hair moved with his rapid thrusts.

I felt him shift and cracked open my eyes, not realizing I had closed them. He moved a hand from one of my thighs to slide it under my ass, then lifted the other hand to my throat. The gentle yet firm squeeze on my neck by his big tattooed hand was exactly what I needed to send me over the edge. I tilted my head back and screamed out my release, not caring at all that the entire club and all the guests at the party could hear me. Nothing mattered but Jack and what he was doing to my body.

As I came down from the most intense orgasm I'd ever had, after-shocks kept sweeping through me. Jack groaned in my ear as my pussy walls kept convulsing. He let go of my throat, sliding his hand around my back, and carried me away from the wall. All I could do was hang on, panting, as he strode over to his desk, each step making his cock move inside me deliciously.

When he reached his desk, he swept out his arm, sending every-thing flying to the floor. He laid me on the surface and then stared down as if he were memorizing the image of me naked and panting for him. With a groan, he pulled his thick cock from my pussy. I immedi-ately reached for him, hating the loss, but my hands met nothing but air as he dropped to his knees on the floor in front of me.

With a jerk, he spread my thighs open wide. The look on his face, as he stared at me with ravenous hunger, had me whimpering as my need grew swiftly again, as if the orgasm that had nearly destroyed my sanity hadn't just ended.

"Fuck," he growled as he moved forward and took a long lick of my wet pussy. "I love the taste of your cunt." He licked me again, then speared his tongue into my entrance. "Never going to stay away from this cunt again. *Mine.*" Then there was no more talking, just grunts coming from him and moans of pleasure from me as he ate me as if he were making up for every day that he hadn't had a taste.

Just as I was about to come again, Jack pulled back, wiping his chin on my thigh. He stood to his feet, towering over me with his cock hard and pulsing with his heartbeat. It was still glistening from being inside me, the tip practically dripping from his precome.

I tilted my head back, an invitation as my neck stretched that he took full advantage of, sliding his hand there as he slid back inside me.

I moaned, feeling complete once again. I lifted my hands to grip his wrist, holding onto him like an anchor. "Jack."

"Never again, Sally."

I opened my eyes to meet his half-lidded gaze as he slid out slowly, then thrust in hard and fast. "Never again," I agreed.

"Fuck! Too good. I'm going to come. *Fuck.*" Jack reached for my breast and pinched my nipple, giving it a hard twist that had me arching my back and my walls clenching around him. "Come with me, little Queen. I want you to squeeze my cock as I fill you up."

I did exactly as he demanded, my whole body freezing and then convulsing as the orgasm took over. I could hear Jack grunt loudly as he pushed deep and then held still as his cock jerked inside me. He draped his body over mine, his face buried in my neck as he let the pleasure sweep through him.

Once we both came down from our orgasms, he withdrew from my body slowly. Then he gently swept me up in his arms. He walked over to the couch with me cradled against him and sat down. He held me against his chest with one arm. With the other, he swept my hair back from my face and then ran his hand over my body. His big, callused hand roamed over my back, arms, and legs, touching every part of me he could reach.

When I shivered from the chill of the room after the way my body had heated during our lovemaking, he reached over to grab the throw blanket he'd bought for me months ago. He tucked it around me, ensuring every part of me was covered. I reached up to stroke his cheek, and he leaned into my palm.

"You're going to make a good dad, Jack."

He stilled at my whispered words. "I'll need you to teach me."

I smiled at him. "You already know how. You take such good care of me. You treat Zero like he's your baby. You won't need me to teach you. But I'll be here to remind you when you need me to."

"Fuck." He pulled me against him, burying his face in my neck again. "I don't deserve you, Sally. I don't deserve any of this happiness you've given me." His words were muttered against my skin, hoarse and full of emotion.

"You deserve everything. Regardless of what you think, you are a good man, Jack. You take care of this town and its people. I've seen how everyone respects you because you treat *them* with respect. You may be gruff and appear mean, but inside, you have the heart of a true hero." I giggled as I teased him. "You're a marshmallow."

He pulled his head back as he narrowed his eyes, looking menacing and dangerous, sending shivers up my spine. I grinned.

"Take it back," he growled.

I shook my head and laughed. "Never."

"Take it back now, woman, or you'll regret it." His tone would have the bravest men trembling in their boots, and they'd be wise to fear Bones, the Devil's Nightmare President. The Nightmare King. But he was my Jack. I booped his nose.

"What will you do to me? Smoother me in kisses?"

I could see the corner of his mouth twitch and knew he was fighting back a grin. His eyes were still narrowed as he tried to glare at me, but there was a lightness there that he so rarely showed.

"Oh, no, little Queen. I'm going to do much worse than that."

Then, all I could do was squeal as I was suddenly lifted and turned, my back meeting the cold leather of the couch. My laughter rang out as his fingers went to my sides. I writhed on the leather as he tortured me with tickles. Not an inch of me was spared as he made sure I was sorry for calling him soft. Once he was satisfied he'd taught me a lesson, he proceeded to show me how much he appreciated my words with more orgasms.

We were too engrossed in each other's bodies and the love we were sharing to care that the bikers of The Devil's Nightmares all grinned at each other as they listened to the laughter and chuckles coming from their President's office. They shared knowing looks, relieved that their King and Queen were back. Then they returned to their party, doing what bikers did best.

JACK

I woke up with a crick in my neck and my bare ass sticking to the leather of the couch in my office. I wondered at first what had woken me until I realized my woman was reaching out, half asleep. Her arm reached into nothingness beyond where I held her tight to my chest. Her arm fell heavy to the base of the couch, startling her into full wakefulness.

She lifted her head, blinking her beautiful, confused blue eyes. "Jack?" The confusion cleared quickly as her eyes took in my face, bouncing from my eyes, my nose, down to my mouth before darting back up to my eyes. A radiant smile broke out over her face. "You're here," she breathed in wonder and relief.

My once dead heart gave an uncomfortable squeeze in my chest. I did that to her. I made her second guess my adoration for her. I tightened my hold across her back and nuzzled into her neck, breathing in the intoxicating fragrance of all that she was. Her scent was mixed with mine. The smell of us together, along with the feel of her sweet, soft body laying snugly against my hard muscles, had my already stiff cock turning hard as stone for her. You would think that I couldn't get hard again so soon after the marathon of sex we'd had the night before. Every surface and most of the walls had seen action last night, but I had learned from the beginning that just the thought of Sally could make me hard over and over again.

"I'm here, baby."

I held her tight and flipped us over in a swift move, grinning when she let out a small squeal of shock at the abrupt movement. I brushed the hair out of her eyes as she blinked up at me, then narrowed her eyes.

"You could warn a girl."

I grinned down at her, then spread my palm over her throat, reaching for her heartbeat. As I found that life force, proof that she was alive, I shifted my hips and slowly sank my cock inside her warm, wet heat carefully, knowing she was likely sore. I watched as her eyes clouded over with pleasure. The sound of her low moan made my heart squeeze for an entirely different reason.

With long, lazy strokes, I brought both of us to a satisfying climax as she ran her hands up and down my back. I could feel her fingers glide softly along the low ridges of the scars. They were nothing like her long, deep ones. The experience I'd had receiving mine was a different kind of torture than what she'd had to endure. We'd both had more traumatizing moments in our lives than most people could even begin to imagine, and it had shaped both of us. It had turned me into a monster that had only learned to feel again once this angel came into my life.

As I emptied myself into her gripping cunt, I buried my face into her neck. The overwhelming emotions threatened to bring tears to eyes that hadn't shed a tear since I held that first blade, feeling it slice through my personal monster's flesh. This woman had somehow brought humanity back to me. I still wasn't sure if I liked that or not. What I did know is that I would never trade her for anything. I would go through a thousand tortures if it led me to my Queen.

"Ummm," she purred as she stretched below me. Once her breathing steadied and her heart rate returned to normal, she whispered, "I love you, Jack."

Would I ever get used to hearing those words? I pressed a kiss to her neck and lifted my head to gaze directly into gorgeous blues. "I love you." My words were like gravel, pushing through a throat tight with emotion. "You are my everything."

Her smile was sweet and soft. She lifted a hand and smoothed it down my cheek, the raspy sound of my thick stubble sounding loud in the quiet office.

"What are we going to do today?"

I slowly withdrew my softened cock from her warmth, already missing the tight grasp of her cunt before I was even all the way out. As I fell out completely, I leaned up on my elbows to glance down her body at where I had been. One of her legs was pressed tightly to the back of the couch, and the other was over the side, spread as wide as she could be in the small space. I watched, fascinated as always, as my release slowly slid from her body.

With a grunt, I smoothed my fingers through the wetness and brought it up to her belly, where my child rested safely. I ran my fingers in slow circles and painted her with my essence. Then I took a finger and wrote four letters through the whole thing.

Once I was done, I looked back up to see her grinning at me. "I guess I'm going to have to wash you up." I looked back down where I had written MINE across her belly. "And because I want to keep those letters on you, I'll have to dirty you up again."

She let out a small laugh. "I think I might have to wait until tomorrow for that." She wiggled her hips and gave a slight wince. "I might be a little sore today."

I wish I could say I felt bad about that. But a part of me felt nothing but pride that I'd fucked my woman so well that she'd feel me even when I wasn't inside her. I got off the couch and held my tattooed hand out to her. "Come on then, little Queen. I'll wash you, then put some ice on your poor, abused cunt."

She blushed as red as her hair as she gripped my hand. "Jack!" Her laughing tone was admonishing, but there was no disguising her small whimper of need as I held her tight against me once we were both standing. I slid my hand down her back, past the lush curve of her ass, and slid further until my thumb was over the puckered hole of her ass, and my fingers were sliding through the wetness of her pussy lips.

I smirked down at her. "Are you sure you want to wait until tomorrow?" I sank a finger into her cunt and swirled my thumb over her asshole. I hadn't taken her there yet, but I would claim all of her one day. She was mine, and I needed to own every single part of her body.

Her little whimper turned into a moan, making my cock, which had finally been satisfied, twitch. Then, a knock sounded at the door, making Sally jump. Her sudden movement made my finger slide deeper. I was about to push back my plans for a shower when Barrel's muffled voice sounded through the door, the tone urgent.

"Sorry, Prez. I hate to interrupt. But, something important has come up that you are going to want to deal with yourself."

"Fuck," I grumbled, watching as Sally's expression went from pleasure to disappointment. With more reluctance than I would have imagined, I pulled my hand from between her legs, giving her one last sweep of my thumb. Her whole body shivered, but she smiled up at me with understanding, already forgiving me for leaving her before I'd even walked out the door. I let out a heavy sigh. "I'm sorry."

She cupped my face and raised up on her toes to press a soft kiss to my mouth. "Don't be, Mr. Biker President. Just be safe for me, okay?"

"Fuck, I don't deserve you." I pulled her tight, drawing her up my body until she wrapped those lithe little legs around my hips. I gripped her hair in my fist and angled her head to give her a proper kiss. It was fast, but it was everything I couldn't find the words to say. I pulled back. "But I'm never letting you go."

"Good," she sighed, letting her legs drop, then stepping back. She looked around the room for her clothes, walking over to where her shirt was peeking out from under my desk. I groaned as she bent over to pick it up, showing off her wet slit. I resisted stroking my cock before walking over to the door, cracking it open just far enough to see Barrel. The tired lines on his face and the tussled hair made it look like he'd enjoyed himself a little too much last night.

I glared at him as he leaned against the doorway. He yawned wide enough for me to see his tonsils, and I was ready to slam the door in his face until he shook his head as if he were shaking away the fatigue. I wondered if he'd even made it to a bed yet. His eyes opened, finally catching sight of my glare, but his gaze went down my body, the smirk that he had pasted on dropping as his mouth gaped open.

"Holy fuck, Prez! Everyone wondered, but no one really thought you'd have the balls to be tattooed literally everywhere."

I heard a snicker coming from behind me and turned my head to see that my girl had most of her clothes on and was pulling her top over her head. She gave me a saucy wink as she strolled over to me, ignoring the scowl I aimed at her for laughing. She walked up behind me and slid her arms around my waist from behind, laying her head on my back before placing a kiss there and poking her head around my arm.

"Hey, Barrel."

He started to give her the signature smirk that he sent all the ladies until I narrowed my eyes in warning. He cleared his throat instead and ran a hand through his messy hair. "Hey, Sally. Morning. Have a good night?"

She laughed softly. "Yeah, it was pretty good. Looks like you didn't get much sleep."

"Nope. There is too much of me to go around. Gotta please all the pretty things, ya know?"

"For fuck's sake. What's the emergency, Barrel?"

He looked back at me, then gestured with a wave of his hand. "Maybe you, uh, should put that thing away before you give me an inferiority complex."

With a grunt, I turned away, striding over to where my jeans lay discarded on the floor. I tugged them on while Sally walked over to the couch and sat down, and Barrel leaned against the doorframe, yawning again.

"What's going on?" I asked while buttoning my jeans. I snagged my T-shirt off the desk chair and pulled it over my head. I needed a shower and hated putting yesterday's clothes back on, but that would have to wait.

He glanced over at where Sally was sitting, watching both of us with interest. "Do you think we should talk in the meeting room?"

I shook my head once. "No. Sally can hear anything you have to say." My tone was final, and there would be no arguments from anyone on the matter. Ever. If anyone disagreed with my Queen being privy to club business, they could get the fuck out. I almost lost her by keeping my distance. I wasn't making that mistake again. Sally was the strongest person I knew. She could handle anything, and I knew she would always stay by my side, no matter what she learned about the club.

Barrel shrugged, seeming to accept my command easily. "Whatever you say, Prez. One of the guys was on patrol and caught one of the Boogeymen in the act of setting one of the warehouses on fire. He's in the shed." He eyed Sally once more. "He may not last long. The fight to subdue him resulted in a few injuries. Had to call Doc in to patch up our member, too. He should be here soon."

Doc was on his way. Good. It was past time to have a talk with him. I needed men I could trust in my inner circle. Men who would have my back, and more importantly, men who would protect my Queen with their lives. I also had a Vice President position I needed to fill.

THE QUEEN OF NIGHTMARES

The knock coming from the office door jerked me awake, and I had a feeling of déjàvu as I looked around the room.

"Sally? Are you in there?" Kara's voice called to me softly through the door, making me sit up. I had a brief moment of nausea as I rose from my lying position, but it passed fairly quickly after I called out to give me a minute.

I realized that I hadn't been sick at all earlier when Jack and I woke up. I had to laugh softly to myself at that. Jack was good for more than just the fantastic orgasms he could give me. He also seemed to help with the morning sickness, too. Now that I thought about it, maybe a lot of the illness had to do with how depressed I was. The mind is a strange thing, and stress can do a lot of damage to a body. At least, I hoped it was that easy, because morning sickness sucked.

After Jack kissed me goodbye, promising that he would be as quick as possible and making me swear not to leave the clubhouse, I went into the restroom and cleaned up as well as I could with the soap and water there. It wasn't the best, and it definitely didn't come close to being shower-clean, but at least I felt fresher than I had when I woke up.

I walked barefoot over to the door and opened it to see Kara standing there with a smile. She looked a lot fresher than I did, obviously having had the shower I was craving. Her long blonde hair was pulled back in a ponytail, and she was wearing a pretty top with a pair of jeans and sneakers.

"Hey, Kara." I swung the door open wider in invitation, and she walked past me after giving me a one-armed hug. I noticed she was carrying a small package about the size of a shoebox.

"Hey, Sally." She sat down on the couch with the box resting on her lap. She looked me up and down critically as if searching for something. "Are you okay?"

I closed the door and sat down on the other end of the couch, turning sideways with one knee bent, my foot tucked under my other leg so I could face her. "Yes? I'm great. Why do you ask?"

"Well, first, I want to apologize. As soon as we walked in, my ex saw me and pulled me away." She bent her head down, looking embarrassed. "We, uh, stayed occupied for most of the night in one of the rooms." She looked me up and down again, her eyes stopping on a few of the fingerprint sized bruises left on my skin from Jack's hands on my upper thighs. "I heard that Bones was super pissed and dragged you back here to his office. I'm so sorry that I got you in trouble. I swear I didn't mean for that to happen."

I laughed at that. "I wasn't in trouble. It's fine. Jack just didn't like that one of the guys got too close to me. Honestly, coming here last night was the best thing I could have done."

Kara cocked her head, looking at me like I was crazy. "Sally, you have bruises. If he's hurting you…"

I waved my hand, cutting off her line of thinking before she could go further. "Jack would never hurt me. I'm a redhead. I bruise like a peach, Kara. Trust me, nothing he did was harmful in any way." I appreciated her concern. I wished that I'd had someone like her when I was growing up and needed someone to care more about my welfare.

I leaned forward and grabbed her hand, giving it a gentle squeeze. "Thank you for being worried about me. I really appreciate it." I let go and sat back against the arm of the couch again. "But, seriously, there is no need for concern about Jack. He loves me."

She let out a gust of air but still didn't look entirely convinced. "Sally, that's what a lot of abused women say. It's easy to make excuses when the person that is abusing you makes you think they are your whole world and that you need them."

My tone was a lot sharper when I replied. "I appreciate your concern. But, as I said, Jack is not abusing me. He treats me like a queen. In fact, he calls me his Queen. He loves me, and," I leaned forward, making sure to emphasize my words, "he does *not* harm me."

She stared at me for a long beat, her expression unreadable. "Okay, Sally," she finally said softly. She stood up after that. "Well, I just wanted to check on you and also to apologize for ghosting you last night." She gave me a smile that seemed a little forced, and I felt bad for being so harsh with her. "I'm really glad you're okay and that it looks like the two of you worked out whatever was going on between you."

"Thanks," I said softly. I stood up to follow her to the door.

As Kara opened the door and started to walk out, she stopped and spun around to face me, holding the box towards me. "Oh! I almost forgot. As I was coming through the gate, the postal guy showed up. I saw that he had this package addressed to you and offered to bring it in."

Surprised, I held out my hands to take the box. I couldn't think of a single reason I would have anything delivered to me, and definitely not at the clubhouse. "That's strange. I haven't ordered anything, and no one I know would send me mail." As I took the box, I was even more confused by how light it was. It almost felt empty.

"Well, maybe Bones ordered you something. Anyway, I've got to go. See you later!" She walked away with a wave.

"Yeah, see you later, Kara." I shut the door and stared at the box as I carried it over to the desk. The shipping label had my name and the address of the clubhouse on it, but I didn't see a sender. The return address was in Pumpkin Patch. "So strange," I murmured. I searched Jack's drawers for a pair of scissors with no luck but grinned when I found a small switchblade. "Typical."

I sliced through the tape and set the knife down, then opened the flaps of the cardboard box, only to see another box inside. The inner box was red and even lighter as I lifted it out. It felt like it was made out of a thin cardstock that could easily be crushed in my hands. There was a strange design on it, making the box look like it was one large die with black skulls instead of dots. I held it up to my ear and shook it gently.

At first, I didn't hear anything and thought that it truly was empty, but then I listened to the faint sound of several small objects bouncing around. I set the box back down with a frown. I didn't have a single solitary clue what it could be. I looked at where the flap was tucked in and reached to lift it. My hand froze for a second as a cold sensation went down my spine. I shook off the feeling of dread, telling myself that I was being ridiculous.

I slid my finger under the edge, sliding the lid out of where it was tucked in, and gripped the thin sides carefully. For a long second, I leaned over and stared into the interior, my mind unable to comprehend what I was seeing. My mind had stalled, maybe from the horror, maybe because what was inside was so unexpected. It wasn't until the insects began to crawl onto my fingers and up my hands that I reacted.

I screamed as my brain finally understood what was happening. In my panic, I brushed my hands against each other, trying desperately to swipe the bugs off me. As I shook my arms frantically, I knocked the box off the desk, the small thud as it hit the floor drowned out by my terrified screeches. I didn't notice more insects escaping the box until I felt them crawling up my legs.

The first bite took me by surprise. I slapped at my thigh, where the pain flared to life. Then I smacked my upper arm, where a second sting lit up my nerve endings. I was shaking, still screaming, and slapping at my body when I felt one on my scalp. I could feel it digging through my hair and immediately bent over to shake it out. I didn't know where to slap anymore. My hands were trembling, and my heart felt like it was going to explode out of my chest when the door flew open.

"What the fuck?" Doc stood stunned for a moment as he took in the scene. Bugs were all over me, crawling under my shirt, in my hair, and even on my face as I jumped around wildly. "Fuck, Sally!"

Doc ran over and immediately began to brush the insects off my arms. He began stomping his heavy shoes, doing a much better job than I had been at squashing anything that fell to the floor.

"Get them off! Get them off me!" I screeched with all the horrified panic I felt as I batted at my hair, shaking my head wildly. It took several long minutes for Doc to free me from most of the insects as I shook and cried.

"What the absolute fuck, Sally! Where did these bugs come from?" he demanded as he stomped on several more creepy crawlies as they tried to scatter once they hit the floor.

"I don't know!" I wailed, still rubbing vigorously at my skin, still feeling the ghostly sensation of a million tiny feet crawling all over me.

"How did they get in here?" His tone was incredulous as he smacked another bug off my shoulder and stomped on it.

I lifted a shaking finger and pointed to the red box that was lying on its side on the floor, now empty. "They were in there. I don't know!" I cried. "A package came addressed to me. When I opened it, they swarmed all over me." I let out a sob and held up my arm so I could look at it. I had red bite marks all over my arm. When I glanced at the rest of my body, I could see I was covered in insect bites. "Oh my god! Doc!"

"Shit. Are you allergic?"

I trembled. "I don't know. I don't even know what those bugs are!"

He pulled me into his body, wrapping a comforting arm around me. I rested my forehead against his chest as I sobbed. I needed Jack. Having Doc hold me was calming my racing heart, but I knew I wouldn't settle until I was in Jack's arms.

"We should get you to the hospital, just in case." He pulled back, peering down at me, "You're pregnant. This kind of trauma might not be good for you." He looked down at the floor to see all the mangled bodies of the bugs. "Fuck. I need one of them so we can identify what they are."

I backed away from the bodies, a shiver racking my body. I didn't want to see another bug as long as I lived. "I don't think anyone could identify any of those," I said with a shudder.

He sighed. "No, I don't think so either."

"Where's Jack?" I tried to keep the whimper out of my voice, but I didn't think I was very successful.

"I'll call him and tell him to meet us at the hospital. Okay?" He put his arm around my shoulders and started to lead me to the door. I spotted my shoes and bent over to slide them on my feet when I felt a tickle under my shirt. My high-pitched scream was loud, bouncing off the walls, as I started jumping around all over again, making it fall to the floor. Doc swiftly grabbed an empty water bottle out of the trash can and scooped the weird looking bug into it before it could escape.

"That'll do," he announced.

JACK

I strode into the shed to see a naked and shivering Boogeyman hanging from the hook in the center of the room. I had to admit, it was pretty cold in the processing room, considering how close it was to Christmas already. There was a furnace for disposing of deer carcasses that came in handy for disposing of other things as well, but it wouldn't be lit for this interaction. Not until later.

I wasn't so sure all the shivering was due to the cold as I stared at the enemy biker. He was scrawny and looked young. He couldn't have been far past twenty. I had no sympathy for his age, however. He made a choice to get in bed with the worst MC in the area. Now, he had to deal with the consequences.

"You don't look so good." I looked him over, taking in all of his injuries, including what looked like a knife wound in his ribs. Barrel was right; the guy wasn't going to last much longer. I needed to get what I could out of him before it was too late.

At the sound of my gravelly voice, his whole body jerked. He slowly lifted his head, revealing an eye swollen shut and a split in his lip, with a watery trail of blood going down past his chin. When he focused his one good eye on me, it widened before he put on a brave front and sneered. Instead of an answer, he spit a wad of blood onto the floor.

"Fuck you, Devil," he croaked out.

I stepped closer. "No thanks. Though, I could have been fucking my woman right now if I didn't have to deal with you. You'll pay for that, too."

"Fuck your whore. Oogie is going to ruin her pussy when he gets ahold of her." He tried to be brave with his foolish words, but the wobble at the end gave away how scared he really was. He was fucked, and he knew it.

Without responding to his taunt, I reared back and punched him in the ribs, right where the knife wound was. His body swayed wildly as his scream echoed around the room.

"Fuck, Prez. That was brutal." Shock winced and rubbed a hand over his own ribcage.

I grunted and walked over to the table already laid out with tools, selecting a long, thin blade typically used for filleting meat. "What do the Boogeymen have planned?" I gritted out as I strolled back over to the young man who had settled into whimpers. His wound was flowing freely with blood, a puddle forming underneath him and rolling into the drain. There was an interesting pattern of blood splatters over the floor where he had swung before one of my men stopped him.

I expected the man to be defiant and tell me to fuck myself again. Instead, he squeezed his eyes shut and whimpered.

"Prez plans to get your woman from behind your walls. He's pissed you built them and made it harder for us to get in." He let his head drop, and his voice was slurred as he continued spilling his secrets as his blood ran thickly from his side and down his leg. "He thinks if he gets the woman, he'll be able to control you. Once he has her, he'll have the town."

He wasn't fucking wrong. I would gladly give up everyone in the town to save my Queen. I ground my teeth so hard my jaw ached, and I could feel a throbbing pain behind my eye from the headache that was forming.

"How does he plan to get her?"

"D-don't know. I just fully patched in last—" he took a breath and then started coughing, blood spraying from his lips. "I'm new, so I don't know anything," he finished in a hoarse whisper.

The kid was almost gone. I wouldn't get anything further from him. I sighed, then swiped across his throat with the knife, making sure to cut deep enough that he would bleed out quickly. His body jerked once before going still. I turned away and dropped the knife on the table for one of the men to clean.

"I shouldn't have to say it, but I'm going to anyway," I said as I looked at each of my men in the eye. These were my closest men, the officers of the Devil's Nightmares, and my inner circle. I trusted them, but I still needed to make sure they understood the seriousness of my words. "Sally is mine. She is to be protected at all costs. She never leaves the compound without me. There needs to be a guard on her location at all times. That means day and night, someone will be guarding my house." I glared at them, daring them to challenge me.

This was new territory for the club. A few members had old ladies, but none that had been under direct threat before. Sally was more than an old lady to me. She was my Queen, and that meant she was Queen of the fucking Nightmares, too.

"She is your Queen. You will protect her and show her the same respect you show me. Is that understood?" I jerked my head and narrowed my eyes to glare at Barrel as he stepped forward.

"Just saying, Prez, but that was a given. We get it." He looked around at the other guys, and they all nodded or grunted their agreement. Shock folded his arms over his chest with a grin on his face. "We're happy for you. We like Red, and we like seeing you happy."

My chest felt strangely warm at his words. As I glanced at each of my inner circle, they all had the same look of agreement and grins. I resisted the urge to rub at my chest. I grunted. "Good." I turned to walk to the door without looking back. I needed to get to my girl after hearing Oogie's plans for her. I would give him whatever he asked for to get her back, but I didn't want him to lay a finger on her. I knew if he did somehow get past me, he wouldn't leave much of her to retrieve. Just the thought alone had cold sweat trickling down my spine.

I punched in the code to the heavy door of the processing room and swung the door open to breathe in the fresh, cold air. Snow was coming soon. The clouds hung heavy and thick in the sky. My breath came in puffs of white as I strolled from the shed to the back of the clubhouse. Before I made it halfway to the main building, the back door flung open, and one of my men came running out. He stopped in his tracks when he saw me. I could clearly read the urgency on his face.

"What's wrong?" I demanded as I quickened my pace.

"It's Sally…"

Before he could finish speaking, I began to run, throwing the heavy back door open hard enough to bang against the wall, and ran down the hall to my office, where I'd left her to wait. The door was standing open, so I pushed inside.

"Sally!" I glanced around the room, not finding my woman. Instead, there was a cardboard box on my desk that hadn't been there before. Red caught my eye, and I looked down to see another box lying on the floor. I blinked at the disgusting mess of insect bodies squashed into the thin carpet.

Before I could turn around to search for my Queen, the same man who had run outside to tell me something about her came into the room, breathing heavily from running.

"Doc took her to the hospital. I don't know what happened. He just told me to find you and tell you to meet him there."

I knew what happened. I walked over to the red box and picked it up, looking inside. There was a bug about the size of a dime that tried to run out and down the side of the red box. I snatched it between my fingers and squeezed. I wiped my hand on the leg of my jeans and plucked the black card out of the bottom of the box.

I tried to do this the easy way, Bones.

I warned you two months ago.

You should have just done what I told you when I left you that message.

Give up the town, or your woman suffers.

This was only the beginning.

I flung the flimsy box to the ground, wishing it was made out of something fragile that would make a satisfying sound as it shattered. As it was, I simply turned away, my need to have Sally in my arms greater than my need to tear the box to pieces. I tucked the small card into my back pocket, then picked up the cardboard box to see a mailing label on it. I turned toward the door, ready to head to my bike. I strode past the man who had come to give me the message and paused just long enough to give him another job to do.

"Give this to Shock. Tell him I want to know who mailed it." I shoved the box at Horse and kept going as he fumbled it until he had a solid grip. "And have the carpet removed from my office. Have them put in a fucking wood floor."

"Got it, Prez. Good luck. Hope she's okay."

I ignored him. She was going to be okay. She fucking had to. But she was also outside the gates without me. If I had to guess, that was precisely the Boogeyman's plan all along. She'd be easy to grab at the hospital. I could only be glad as fuck that Doc was with her. If there was one person I could count on to protect her almost as well as I could, it was my brother.

Just because she belonged to me would have been enough for him to want to, but I knew that he had a soft spot for my girl. He had checked on her several times over the past few months. From the time she had first moved in with me after her attack in the alley and then after she'd nearly lost her arm, he always made sure to check on her to see how she was healing. After I was done ensuring my girl was going to be okay, I would be giving my brother a demand that he wouldn't be able to refuse this time.

I let the heavy steel door at the front of the clubhouse slam closed with a bang and strode to my bike. I heard steps from heavy boots running in my direction. Without pausing my long strides, I called out to Barrel.

"I'm heading to the hospital. Send out a message to every club member. I want all exits to Pumpkin Patch covered. If any Boogeymen are spotted, I want them captured for interrogation."

I heard the steps slow, then pick back up again as they headed in the opposite direction. I knew Barrel would likely be pissed that he wasn't coming with me, but I needed him to get the town protected and locked down more than I needed a shadow. Ever since Lock was murdered, Barrel had been determined to become my personal bodyguard. His way of working through grief, I supposed, but he would understand my need for the order.

With a command for Zero to stay behind as he trotted up to me with a whine, I straddled my Harley, then took off with a deafening roar of the engine and a cloud of dust.

THE QUEEN OF NIGHTMARES

Doc was exasperating. From the time we'd left Jack's office, he had been fussing over me. He had already asked me how I felt no less than ten times in the fifteen-minute drive. And now he was trying to convince me to let him carry me into the hospital. I could see the worry written all over his face, though, so I could forgive him. But I still wasn't going to let him carry me.

"Doc, it's just some bug bites! What's the worst that could happen? I scratch until I bleed?" I turned and started following the signs that guided me toward the emergency entrance to the hospital. I felt a little silly for going to the ER for bug bites. If it weren't for my worry about the baby I was carrying, I probably would have just covered myself in Benadryl cream and taken some Tylenol.

"Anaphylaxis, necrosis, death."

His words spoken so matter of fact had me pausing. I swallowed hard before turning to look over my shoulder as he caught up with me.

"Isn't it past time to be worried about anaphylaxis?" I blinked up at him, picking out the features that he shared with Jack as a way to calm my sudden burst of nerves.

He sighed and put his arm around my shoulder, leading me over to a side entrance I hadn't noticed. "Yes. But there's still time to have a negative reaction. And necrosis could take a few days to start showing up." He pulled a card out of his wallet and scanned it before pulling the door open. He guided me inside the brightly lit hallway, straight to the busy desk in the center of the large room the hallway opened up into.

The nurse who sat behind the desk, typing away on a keyboard, asked in a tired, bored voice, "Can I help you?" before looking up. I had to bite down on both lips to stop myself from giggling at the double-take the pretty brunette did once she realized who was standing at her desk. Her entire demeanor changed from the harried, overworked nurse to a shy, blushing schoolgirl.

"Dr. Erickson." Her cheeks turned rosy, and I could see how hard she was clenching the arms of her chair. But what really caught my eye was the way Doc's eyes seemed to soften as he glanced down at her.

"Helen." His tone was unlike anything I'd ever heard come from him. His two default tones tended to be gruff and sarcastic. Hearing him speaking so softly and gently had my eyes widening in shock. Doc's hand that was still on my shoulder squeezed. "This is my sister-in-law, Sally. She got into some kind of bug nest and was bit quite a few times."

With a concentrated effort, Helen tore her eyes away from Doc's handsome face and looked me over. Seeing her own eyes widen at all the red, swollen bumps covering my scarred flesh had me ducking my head, ready to hide in a way I hadn't since Jack had come into my life and made me believe I was beautiful. To the nurse's credit, she didn't act like I was strange for wearing the stupid shorts and top in the freezing cold weather. I wished I had thought to ask to stop by the house for a quick change of clothes first.

"Usually, I would advise a patient to watch and wait with a dose of Benadryl. But Sally is pregnant." His jaw clenched as he got pissed off all over again at the memory of seeing me covered in crawling, biting insects. "My brother would be a little upset if anything happened to his girl." I grimaced. That was the understatement of the century. The last time someone had hurt me, Jack settled for destroying his ability to walk, only because he had witnesses and couldn't pull the trigger without ending up in prison. "So, I'm going to need full panels done as well as an ultrasound machine to check on the baby."

Helen stood up quickly. The brief flare of what I thought I recognized as jealousy was wiped clean and replaced by sympathy by the time Doc finished speaking. "Of course! I believe room seven is open. I'll go run and check. Just wait here."

I watched the pretty nurse speed walk down a hall, then turned to look up at Doc with a raised eyebrow. "Helen, huh?"

He turned his gaze from the direction she had disappeared and narrowed his dark eyes on me. Though more rich chocolate and less deep, bottomless abyss, Doc's eyes still reminded me of Jack. I wasn't exactly sure what it was about them. "Don't," he growled. I would have pushed him just for the fun of it, but Helen was already returning.

"Your room is ready for you, Sally. If you'll follow me, I can get you set up."

I looked back at Doc for a second, but his eyes were glued to a different woman, and I couldn't catch his eye. I didn't want to be left alone, even if I was in a hospital. It just seemed like a bad idea after what had happened today. Being here at all could be playing right into the person's hands. When I heard the footsteps coming, I let out a sigh of relief that he wasn't going to leave me alone.

"What kind of insects were they?"

The softly spoken question jarred me from my thoughts but brought me back to the feeling of all those creepy crawlies. I clenched my fist to keep from patting my hair for any strays. Again.

"Uh, I have no idea. Doc?" We both looked over our shoulders to see Doc jerk his eyes up from the general location of where our asses had been. I smirked as he cleared his throat.

"What?"

"Where's the bug you managed to save?"

"Shit. I left it in the truck. I'm going to need to run and get that. But it can wait until Bones gets here first."

I gave him a grateful smile and then turned to the nurse. "It was about an inch long, maybe less, and was brown. It had a lot of legs like a millipede, but it definitely wasn't as long, maybe more like a pill bug, only hairy instead of body armor. Oh," I winced as I gave in to the increasing urge to scratch one of the many bites."They bite or pinch or sting. I know that's not helpful. I'm sorry."

"Have you tried Googling the bug?" she asked, and I shook my head.

"It all happened so fast. I didn't even grab my phone before heading here."

Doc spoke up, already pulling his phone out of his pocket. "I'll start looking while you get dressed in the hospital gown. I'll be right outside the room, so don't worry." I nodded, my neck feeling stiff, and my smile was brittle as I followed Helen into the room.

She walked over to a cabinet and pulled a typical gown from a shelf before handing it to me. "Change into this. I'm assuming Dr. Erickson will be the one to run your tests, so I'll wait for him to give his instructions. I will get your ultrasound machine ordered, though." She smiled as she walked to the door and pulled the curtain toward the wall, blocking all view inside the room from the open door, before closing the door behind her.

I had the top and shorts I had been wearing off and folded neatly on the chair before struggling with the ties on the hospital gown. Suddenly, I was hot, sweaty, and finally feeling that nausea I hadn't missed waking up with this morning. It seemed that whatever charm Jack had for holding back the morning sickness had worn off.

I collapsed back on the bed and breathed deeply with my eyes closed. I wasn't sure if I was going to make it without having to sprint for the toilet. I heard the heavy knock on the door and swallowed thickly. "Come in," I croaked out before the wooden door swung inwards.

"You decent, Red?"

I grunted out my answer. I rolled up one hip to tug on the blanket I was lying on, barely having the energy.

"Hey, hey. What's going on? You were fine a minute ago?"

"I feel sick. And hot." I whined with a ridiculous pout as I felt sorry for myself.

"Come on. Get up so I can fix your sheets. Bones should be here in just a few minutes. Then you can get my brother to rub your back or whatever shit will make you feel better." I snorted as I lowered my feet back to the cold floor.

"Nice bedside manner you have there, *Dr. Erickson*," I swayed, and the room seemed to grow smaller as I watched through squinted eyes as Doc pulled the blanket and sheet back for me.

"Family and the club get the real me. The hospital gets the professional me. Don't you feel special?" He turned to look at me after I had stayed silent. I was patting my clammy cheek and taking in deep breaths through my nose.

"Oh, shit." Doc darted to the sink to grab a plastic bag attached to a bottomless cup from the small stack sitting there. With expert ease, he had the long blue bag stretched out and the cup shoved under my chin just in time.

I groaned once I was done. It probably wouldn't have been so bad if I had at least eaten something. But after Jack left, I had fallen back to sleep. Then Kara woke me up, and after that, the whole bug thing happened.

Heavy footsteps sounded outside in the corridor, seconds before my heavy room door was pushed open. I knew it was Jack before he even came around the curtain, but I was surprised to see Doc holding a gun and holding me back with his arm when I tried to get past him to get to Jack.

"Jack!" His name came out in a strangled sob. All of the emotions I had been trying to hold back, all the fear, pain, the sudden weakness from being sick. It all came out of me as Jack shoved past Doc when he didn't move back quickly enough. He scooped me up in his arms and held me cradled to his chest, giving a grateful nod of thanks to his brother before Doc slipped out the door. Without a word, he let me get it all out until I gave an exhausted hiccup.

Jack rested his cheek on the top of my head. "I'm so sorry I wasn't there for you."

I let out a shaky breath, then cringed. "You have nothing to feel bad about Jack." I covered my mouth with my hand. "But, if you love me, you will take me to the sink so I can rinse out my mouth. I kinda threw up right before you showed up."

He cursed as he stood up and carried me to the sink. He handed me a small paper cup and turned on the cold water. "I didn't get your ginger cookies and tea this morning."

I spat out the water and glared into Jack's beautiful dark eyes before turning back to the sink and rinsing again. When I spit it out, I reached for a paper towel, smacking Jack's hand away when he tried to do it for me.

"You can't control the world, no matter how big, bad, and tough you are. You just have to accept that some things you can't command and deal with the aftermath the way we mere mortals have had to do our entire lives."

"I don't like seeing you sick or injured," he growled as he walked me back over to the hospital bed. Then he sat down on the edge, swinging his legs up so he could rest comfortably against the raised head with me in his arms.

"I'm certain I wouldn't like seeing you hurt either, Jack. But if that were to happen, I would do everything I could to help you get better."

He raised a sexy eyebrow and ran his tattooed fingers over the red, swollen bites on my cheeks. While he inspected the bites, I ran a fingertip over his neck, lightly tracing the bones that were shaded so spectacularly. I couldn't help but admire the artistic talent. His T-shirt covered the base of his neck down, so I wasn't able to give into the enjoyment of tracing the rest of the bones down his chest.

"You wouldn't torture yourself with the thought that there might have been something you could have done to prevent it?"

I huffed. "I don't see why we have to play the semantics game."

Jack snorted, then kissed the tip of my nose. "Right. Semantics."

I tapped my fingertip on his stubbled chin and gave a decisive nod. "Thank you for seeing things my way, sir."

THE QUEEN OF NIGHTMARES

A knock on the door had Jack and I looking in that direction as if we held the ability to see through the fabric hanging in the way. The door cracked open just before the familiar voice of Helen called out. I covered Jack's hand with my own, giving a shake of my head so he'd slide the gun back under his vest before the sweet nurse that his brother had a crush on could see it and freak the fuck out.

"Hey, Sally. Dr. Erickson said his brother arrived." She was dragging something on wheels, and I saw her backside before the rest of her came into view.

I nudged Jack. "Go help her."

He didn't say a word; he just tightened his arms around me. Which I suppose was answer enough. Jack wasn't ready to let me go yet.

"Oh my." Helen's words trailed off once she caught sight of Jack holding me possessively in his arms. She looked away quickly as if she had caught us in a compromising position that wasn't as innocent as him holding me tightly with all our clothing on. Well, I mean, I was in just a thin gown with my ass completely exposed.

"I have the ultrasound machine here. I told the technician I would get it set up for them, but they should be here in just a few minutes," Her rambling was cute, but I didn't like the idea that I was making her uncomfortable. I nudge Jack again.

"Maybe you should let me up."

Again, he tightened his arms. "I can't, Sally. Don't ask me again."

"Oh, please don't get up if you're comfortable. It's okay." Helen gave a reassuring smile as she glanced over from where she had begun to sort wires and plugs for the big square machine.

"It's you I don't want to make uncomfortable. Jack can hold my hand from the chair." I stared pointedly at Jack as I said the words. He stared right back at me blankly.

Helen stopped prepping and turned to look us over again. "You don't make me uncomfortable. You make me wistful. I wish I had what you two so clearly do." She hit a button on the machine, and the screen came to life. "It might be a little jealousy, too." She laughed lightly, then walked back to the door. "I'll see you two soon. And don't worry, Dr. Erickson's brother, I'll inform the ultrasound tech that she needs to expect her patient to be held while she does her job." She gave a wink and a smile before pausing at the door. "She can work around you." With that, she was gone.

"What's going on with that nurse?" Jack jerked his chin in the direction of the now empty doorway.

"I think Doc has a crush on her. Or she has a crush on him? Maybe a mutual crush." I shrugged. "But it was clear they both liked each other. It's also clear that neither one of them has acted on it." I turned on Jack's lap to face him more. "Do you think—"

"No." His tone was flat. Final.

"But, Jack—"

"No."

I gave out a disgruntled huff and crossed my arms over my chest. I wasn't going to agree not to meddle, no matter what Jack said. What could it hurt to give a little push?

"Little Queen," his tone was a warning, but I could hear the amusement he was failing to hide. I just gave a non-committal hum as I stared at the floral pattern on the curtain. Jack sighed and settled his chin on my shoulder. I absentmindedly scratched at the spots on my arms. The bites weren't too bad, but they were definitely itchy.

A large hand settled over mine, stopping my fingernails from doing any damage. "Baby, I don't want you to make yourself bleed. I'm barely holding it together here. If I see blood on your beautiful skin, I'm going to start tearing things apart."

I sighed and snuggled further into his warm body. I relaxed into him and allowed his comforting presence to soothe away the lingering terror. I let my eyes drift shut and let my mind wander back to last night and our conversation. Before the attack a couple of months ago, I had been the happiest I had ever been in my life. It was difficult just to erase all the pain and doubt that I had gone through in the recent weeks, but knowing that all of our problems stemmed from a lack of communication had gone a long way in making me get past it. We just needed to avoid anything like it in the future.

It wasn't long before another knock sounded on the door. It opened immediately, a feminine voice calling from behind the curtain.

"Sally? Are you ready for your sonogram?"

A small woman with a bright smile and a headful of long, shiny braids twisted back into a smooth updo stepped around the curtain at my answering, "Yes."

"Great! I'm Shana." She walked over to the machine that Helen had set up and started clicking on the multitude of buttons. "Helen warned me that we might have to do this with company." She grinned, eyeing Jack's arms that were still wrapped tight around me. "I don't blame you." She winked and held out a skinny white bottle. "But I'm going to need you as flat as possible."

With some maneuvering, I wiggled until I was flat on my back, my head in Jack's lap. My feet were hanging off the end of the bed, but the ultrasound technician didn't seem to mind the position I had to get into to keep Jack from losing his shit. When I lifted my gown up to tuck under my breasts, Jack made sure to keep my lower half covered while holding one arm over my breasts. His overprotectiveness had me wondering how he would react once it was time for me to deliver this baby. If he didn't want to see me in pain, he was going to be in for a rude awakening in a few more months.

"Okay, here we go. It's warm, so it shouldn't be too much of a shock." Shana leaned over, squirted a large glob of the jelly substance over my lower belly, and then placed the doppler on my skin. It wasn't unpleasant, just a strange sensation that made me want to squirm.

All thoughts of weird jelly-like substances and exposed flesh flew from my mind as soon as the staticky sounds from the machine evened out into a steady beating. My breath caught at the sound, and Jack's arm tightened around me.

"There we are," Shana murmured quietly and used one hand to shift dials and press buttons while holding the wand steady. She shifted the wand a little and held still before shifting again. "It looks like your little bean is doing good. Heartbeat is nice and strong." She turned the screen so I wouldn't have to crane my neck. There, in a pool of black and white, was a small image of a heart beating wildly. "It isn't always easy to see the fetus this early in your pregnancy, but this is a great shot."

She spoke some more, but I couldn't focus on her words. All I could do was stare at the beautiful sight of the little heart fluttering. "Jack," I whispered in awe, reaching up and grabbing onto his hand.

"I see it, little Queen." His voice was gruff with the emotions he was holding in. "I love you." He whispered the words into my hair, and we both took in the moment we saw our baby and heard the heartbeat for the first time. I blinked back the tears that threatened to cloud my vision. I didn't want to miss a single second of this moment.

After several more minutes of tapping buttons and moving the wand around, Shana removed the doppler and smiled down at me. "I'll send the images to the doctor, but it looks like everything is right on track for your estimated date of conception." She handed me a towel and started cleaning up the doppler. "Congratulations!"

I gave her a watery smile as I swiped the towel over the gel on my abdomen. "Thank you."

"There's only one in there, right?" It was the first time I thought I'd ever heard Jack sound hesitant, but the girl laughed.

"Only one." She winked as she held out a strip of paper to Jack. He took it gingerly in his big, tattooed hand. I tilted my head back to see what he was holding but got stuck on the absolute awe on his face as he stared down at the images of our baby. Seeing Jack fall in love with our baby made my heart feel like it was swelling with more love than I could possibly contain.

Shana slipped out of the room quietly as we both stared at the grainy images. "I'm going to be the best father I can, Sally. I promise."

I turned in the bed and crawled back up to rest against his chest again. His arms wrapped around me, holding me close, his chin on my shoulder.

"I know you will, Jack. You're going to be an amazing father."

He tore his eyes from the pictures to gaze down at me as I tilted my head up to look at his handsome face. "Thank you."

I shrugged and gave him a lopsided smile. "It's the truth."

"No. I mean, thank you for giving me what I never thought I could have. Until you came into my life, I was barely living. I had my club, my bike, and my dog. Now, I have everything."

"Jack," I cupped his cheek and let out a breath heavy with emotion. "It's you that gave me hope for a better life. I was dead inside after what I had gone through. I was in constant fear, always wondering if I would ever be able to walk outside and not be afraid. I didn't know if I would ever be able to find a way to live again. You gave me back my life. You make me feel safe, loved, and cherished."

He closed his eyes and leaned into my touch before opening his dark eyes again. He looked deep into my soul. "We brought each other to life."

"Yes." His lips touched mine in a soft caress. His kiss was gentle, reverent.

"Marry me."

The words were whispered against my lips, and it took a long second for them to penetrate. I pulled back and stared up at him, eyes wide. My gaze took him in, seeing his fierce determination, the firm set to his jaw. I searched for any signs of regret that the words had come out of him. The longer I stared, the narrower his gaze became until he was glaring at me.

"You *will* marry me."

I let out a breathless laugh. "Are you sure?"

He let out a growl before grabbing me by the hips and turning me to face him on the hospital bed. His hands were tight, just shy of bruising, as he crushed me to him. His mouth took mine in the type of brutal kiss I was used to from him, making me melt against his hard chest. When he broke the kiss, he glared at me some more.

"I'm not asking. You are my woman, my Queen. You are going to marry me and make me the happiest fucking biker there has ever been, or I will put you over my knee and spank your ass until you do."

I burst into tears again for the hundredth time that day and threw my arms around his shoulders as I cried into his neck. He held me tight against him, rubbing my back as I let out the last bit of anxiety I'd been holding on to.

That was how Doc found us when he walked into the room a few minutes later. He stood there with a bemused look on his face, staring at the emotional mess I was, when Jack decided to announce loudly that Doc would be his best man and the club's Vice President—whether he liked it or not.

THE QUEEN OF NIGHTMARES

After Jack's declaration said in a tone full of stark finality coupled with a glare, daring Doc to argue, he and Doc stepped outside the room for a quiet discussion. Before leaving, Jack kissed me lightly on the lips and gave my still flat belly a gentle rub. He let me know that he was planning to run to the cafeteria for some terrible coffee, but there would be a prospect standing guard outside the room just in case the Boogeymen tried to make a move. At this point, it seemed unlikely, but the chance of an attack couldn't be eliminated completely, and I couldn't deny that having someone there made me feel better.

I lay in the bed, trying desperately not to scratch at the itchy spots, and waited for the Benadryl to kick in. Doc had assured both of us that it would be perfectly safe to take. Even so, Jack did a quick internet search to verify for himself while Doc stood by the door, glaring with his arms crossed over his chest. I had to smile, even as I rolled my eyes for Doc's benefit at Jack's overprotectiveness. The brothers were more alike than either of them realized.

I wanted to go home. I hated being in the hospital after what I had experienced at the hands of Dr. Stein. Just being in the building brought back horrible memories. More than once, the man had sent me to the hospital. But Doc wanted to ensure that everything looked good before we could go, so he refused to allow me to leave until the lab processed my bloodwork.

I was staring at the deep, red scar that ran across the upper part of my forearm when the door to the room opened again. There was no knock, so I had assumed it was Jack returning already, but whoever it was entering was quiet and definitely not my biker President.

A thin, young woman wearing blue scrubs edged around the curtain as I eyed her. She had her head down, her short, dark hair concealing her face as she slowly walked toward the machine to my left that was monitoring my heart rate. I watched warily, wondering why she was acting so strangely.

My phone began to vibrate on the bed next to me. Jack had placed it there when he first showed up. He'd wanted me to keep it close in case I needed to reach him, not happy that I had left it behind at the clubhouse. The ringing distracted me from the quiet nurse. When I glanced down at it, I saw an unknown number from California. With a frown, I declined the call, figuring it was a sales call or something equally unimportant from my time living there.

I glanced back up to see the nurse staring at me from the corner of her eye. It was obvious she wasn't there to take notes on my vitals. My hand moved to the call button on the side of the bed when she finally turned to look at me, a desperate look on her face.

"Please, don't."

I knew that voice. The woman looked different without the pink hair and the arrogant attitude, but there was no mistaking who it was.

"Daisy." I picked my phone up, already preparing to call Jack, when she reached over and snatched the phone from my hand.

"Sally, please listen to me!" she begged in a desperate whisper, eyeing the curtain that was concealing the door.

I glared up at Daisy. I could admit that I was shocked to see her standing in front of me, alive and well. A part of me had expected Jack to kill her. She had been a spy, after all. The last time I had seen her, she had taunted him to kill her as she spewed toxic venom at him. The threats she made about her brother and what he was planning on doing to me would have been enough to have Jack end her life. So, seeing her standing in my hospital room alive and apparently doing well had my head spinning.

"What are you doing here?" I demanded, eyeing the phone she now held in her hand. I glanced at the door, knowing all I needed to do was yell out to have the Nightmare prospect running inside.

Daisy glanced toward the door again and swallowed before slowly reaching out to hand my phone back to me. "I owe Bones my life. I need to repay him."

I opened my mouth to respond, but no words came out. I realized I should have asked questions back then, but I had thought at the time it was best I didn't think of Jack as a woman murderer. Even if I could understand his reasonings, it would have been difficult to reconcile the act with the man I had come to love. Now, it seemed there was a lot more to the man than I ever could have imagined.

Daisy gestured to the phone I was holding with a trembling hand. "I understand if you want to call him, but I hope you'll give me a few minutes to explain."

I eyed her, really taking her in. She looked the same, but there were subtle differences. The thick makeup was gone, allowing her natural beauty to shine. Her hair was dark in what I assumed was her natural shade, making her pretty eyes pop with color. She looked healthy, even if she seemed spooked.

"You have five minutes," I threatened, setting the phone in my lap and eyeing her with my best no-nonsense stare.

She gave me a small smile that wobbled just a little. "Thank you," she whispered. "Bones gave me enough money to disappear after I told him everything I knew about what my brother had planned for the Devil's Nightmares. I took the money and got on the first bus out of town. I made it to Tennessee, where I rented a small apartment and got a job at a bar." She shrugged a shoulder and gave a self-deprecating smile. "It's all I really know how to do."

She sighed, rubbing her forehead before continuing. "Anyway, I have a cousin back here that I was worried about, so I decided to call her, making her promise not to let Oogie know I was alive. I've been hiding with her while I tried to figure out a way to get a message to you." She paused and stared at me with a serious expression. "I found out that Oogie has someone else spying on the Nightmares."

I inhaled sharply at the news. With all the security Jack had been implementing and the plans they were making to take out the Boogeymen, it could mean disaster for everyone if there was another mole in the club. If they knew too much, it could mean death for everyone.

"Who is it?"

She was already shaking her head before I could get the words out. "I don't know. I wish I did, really. But Cherise didn't know either. She just overheard her old man talking about it with some of the guys who had come over for drinks one night. Cherise thought I was dead, too, and had been pissed at Oogie for putting me in the position in the first place, knowing what would happen if I were caught." She shook her head. "I should never have agreed to do it. I knew it was dangerous and that I probably wouldn't make it out alive, but Oogie has a way of forcing the issue.

"When I told Cherise about what Bones did for me, she insisted on telling me what she could, hoping to help. Sally," she looked at me with big eyes, "please know, not everyone is like my brother. Most of us don't agree with how he runs the club or the other horrible things he does." She shuddered and looked across the room to the window overlooking the town of Pumpkin Patch. The lights outside twinkled with the strange mix of Christmas and Halloween that the town seemed to thrive on. With Christmas just around the corner, the pumpkins decorating the town were more jovial than menacing, and much of the pumpkin artwork adorning the shop windows had Santa hats and other Christmas-themed items added.

"I can't stay," she said, glancing back at me. "Bones said if I ever returned, he wouldn't hesitate to kill me this time. I really can't blame him. But I needed to warn you. I couldn't find a way to get to you after the fences were put up around the compound."

"Are you the one that sent the box of insects to me?"

She looked shocked and took a step back, almost hitting the wall behind her. "No! I swear it wasn't me. It's something Oogie would do, though. He loves to terrorize." She got a faraway look in her eye and shuddered again as if remembering her own torment at her brother's hands. "I just heard that you were here. The town likes to talk, and gossip travels fast. I thought it would be my best chance to let you know." She stared at me, her look intense and serious. "Sally, he plans to take you. I didn't know how true my words were when I was threatening Bones that day, but my brother really does plan to take you. He thinks if he can get to you, he'll be able to control Bones and force him to give up the club and town. If Bones is no longer the President, he will be able to take down the entire club. You have to keep an eye out at all times. Someone close to you is working for him. You can't trust anyone."

Heavy footsteps could be heard outside the door, and both of our heads jerked in that direction. "Shit," she hissed and darted her eyes around frantically.

I made a split-second decision. "Quickly! Go into the bathroom!" I waved her in the direction of the open door. "I'll find a way to get you out of here, I promise."

She took a couple of steps toward the bathroom, stopped, and came back over to me with tears in her eyes. "Thank you, Sally. I really am sorry for everything. In case you ever need me." Then she turned and darted into the small room right before the door opened. I closed my hand over the small slip of paper she had placed in my lap.

I quickly thought of how I should handle the situation. I hated lying to Jack or keeping secrets from him, but even though I had little reason to, I believed Daisy. She was putting her life on the line to save mine, and that made me trust her. There was a good chance that Jack would react violently to having someone who used to be such a threat so close to me, especially after what happened today.

As Jack stepped around the curtain while holding a paper cup in both hands, I smiled. He really was a good man. Better than anyone knew. He could have killed Daisy; instead, he gave her a new life. It made my heart swell with love for him even more than I already had.

"Hey, little Queen. I got you some hot tea." He set the cup down on the table before leaning over to kiss the top of my head.

I closed my eyes, savoring the warmth of his breath on me as he lingered there. When I opened them, I glanced at the closed bathroom door. I needed to protect him as much as I did Daisy. I couldn't allow him to hurt her. And he would in a heartbeat if he thought I needed protecting, but if he did, his conscience would forever eat away at him.

"Jack?" I asked in a quiet voice.

"Hmmm?" He ran the backs of his tattooed fingers over my cheek, and I leaned into them.

"I'm a little hungry. Do you think that you can get me something small to eat? Maybe a sandwich? Or a muffin?" I looked up at him to see he was already straightening to his full height, ready to go get me whatever I asked for. It had my conscience pricking at me. I hesitated. "Maybe one of the guys could go get it for me?"

He shook his head. "I'll get you what you need, baby. Is turkey okay?"

I blinked back the tears that started stinging my eyes at his thoughtfulness. "Turkey would be perfect."

"Good. I'll be back before you know it. If you need me for any reason, call." He tapped the phone in my lap and bent down one last time to kiss me as I lifted my chin to meet his lips.

"Thank you," I whispered.

"Don't thank me for taking care of you, little Queen," he said before heading back out of the room.

After several long seconds, Daisy cracked the bathroom door open, peeking her head out. Without another word to each other, we both nodded and then she followed quietly behind Jack. I didn't know if I would ever see her again, but I wished her well and silently thanked her for risking everything just to bring me a warning.

THE QUEEN OF NIGHTMARES

It was late before we finally made it back home. My bloodwork had come back clean, with no serious concerns for my health. Doc had insisted on a final ultrasound right before we left the hospital to check on the baby one last time. It was clear that he was going to be an overprotective uncle. I was already starting to tease him about it. He was still arguing with Jack about becoming the new Vice President, but I was certain that Jack would get his way.

Doc found an entomologist to send the bug to at a nearby university, though it didn't seem to matter at that point. The inflamed bites had lessened in swelling with the dose of Benadryl he had prescribed at the hospital. It seemed whatever they were, it wasn't venomous. The entomologist didn't seem concerned about the insect when he saw the picture but promised he would look at it closer once he received the body. It was a lesson I would never forget, though. I won't be taking any more chances on unknown packages in the future.

I collapsed on the couch, exhausted from the day, even though I had spent the majority of it in a hospital bed. Jack dropped his keys on the table by the front door after waving off Doc, who had given me a ride back in his SUV. He locked the door and set the alarm before turning to look at me. Zero and I were huddled together with his fluffy white head in my lap as he stared up at Jack with baleful eyes. I had a feeling he could sense that something had happened. Either that, or he just didn't like how I had left him all alone all day after the last couple of months being available for cuddles any time he wanted.

Jack snorted, then shook his head as he shrugged off his leather cut. He folded it and laid it over the arm of the recliner adjacent to the couch. He sat down and then started removing his heavy motorcycle boots. I couldn't tear my eyes away from the sight of his muscles bunching and moving under the black T-shirt he wore. It never failed to send a thrill through me when I watched him. He was so beautiful.

Once he tugged off his socks, laying them over the tops of his boots, he stood back up and disappeared in the direction of the kitchen. I closed my eyes as I listened to him moving around. It was so strange to think that this was my life now. I never could have imagined being here just a few short months ago. But as I dug my fingertips into Zero's thick fur, I relished every second.

Jack came back into the room with a bottle of beer and a water bottle. I gave him a smile when he handed me the water, then giggled at Zero's disgruntled huff when Jack shooed him off the couch, taking his place at my side. Jack's arm went around me, pulling me close, and we both sighed at the contact.

"Did you know you had voicemails?" He asked as he pulled my phone out of my pocket, about to toss it onto the coffee table.

"Hmmm?" I was sleepy, ready to end the night after such a long day. "Oh. I forgot. I was getting spam calls all day, I think." I frowned down at the phone he held toward me. "I didn't recognize the number, so I didn't pay attention to it."

He hesitated, then pushed the phone into my hand. "You should check, just in case," he suggested, "unless you want me to check for you."

I shrugged. "I doubt the Boogeymen are calling me from a California number." After unlocking the phone, I went to the voicemails, ready to delete them without looking, when the words of the first message caught my eye. My breath seized.

Jack tensed at my reaction, then slipped the phone from my suddenly trembling fingers. His vicious curse had me squeezing my eyes closed. He put the voicemail on speaker, and we listened to it together.

"Miss O'Hara? This is Marshall Douglas from the California State Penitentiary in Los Angeles County. I have been trying to reach you regarding a very serious matter that may be a cause for concern for your safety. As of 8:37 am this morning, the inmate by the name of Finkle Stein escaped the custody of his correctional officers during a routine doctor's visit. It is believed the prisoner exaggerated his inability to walk. At this time, we have no known location for his whereabouts. We feel you should be on high alert as we conduct our search for Finkle Stein. For any additional information, you can reach my office at 555-691-0102."

Once the voicemail ended, Jack played the second one that said much the same information. All I could do was sit there in stunned disbelief. How could it have happened? I was too out of it at the time, but it was my understanding that Jack had broken the doctor's knees so severely that he was never supposed to walk again. Dr. Stein was never supposed to be a threat to me or anyone else after going to prison.

Stunned, I stumbled up from the couch, refusing to listen to any more of the messages that were a warning to my safety. There was no doubt he was going to come for me. On stiff legs, I walked down the hallway, ignoring Jack's curses. By the time I made it to the bedroom, I was gasping for breath. My arm was throbbing painfully, the ache there vicious as the phantom feeling of the knife that had torn through my skin and muscle began its torturous slicing all over again.

I stumbled against the bathroom counter, my hand catching me before I could fall against the tile. My head was ringing with my own screams. *No. No. No.* He wasn't supposed to leave prison. I didn't have to testify against him because he was caught red-handed, literally, holding the knife. He had been sentenced to life. I was supposed to be free.

I rushed to the toilet, dropping to the floor. As I emptied my stomach, Jack gathered my hair. He knelt beside me, not saying a word. As I slumped over the toilet seat and blinked up at him through watery eyes, I could see what it was costing him to remain strong for me.

Jack was the kind of man that wanted to slay my demons. If he could, he would hunt down Dr. Stein and destroy him once and for all. I knew he had to be beating himself up inside, thinking that he had failed me.

"Jack," my voice was a croak as I reached out to him.

He took my fingers in his, shaking his head. He helped me to my feet and led me over to the counter, lifting me and then setting me on the cold tile. His jaw was locked tight, the muscles there bunched and straining under the pressure. I tried to reach for him again, but he stepped back from my grasp, instead turning to grab my toothbrush, readying it for me.

"Please," I hiccuped.

"I'm sorry," he ground out.

"It's not your fault, Jack." My voice was a plea. I desperately wanted Jack to hold me, to tell me everything would be okay. But I knew it wouldn't be that easy.

"I should have fucking killed him!" He finally shouted after I finished rinsing the toothpaste from my mouth.

"If you had, then you would be the one in prison." My gentle reminder did nothing to calm the rage burning in his eyes.

He finally looked at me and ran a fingertip over my lips as I fought my own internal battle between my fear and the need to keep Jack calm. "But, then, you would be safe, little Queen."

I shook my head. "From one monster, maybe. But what about the rest of them? I need you here, with me. I need you to be my hero."

He gave a derisive snort as he scooped me back into his arms and carried me to our bed. "I've never been anyone's hero, baby."

"You're mine," I whispered, thinking of all he had done for so many people. The way he protects the town. The way he refused to kill Daisy after everything she had done. "You are more a hero than you could possibly know, Jack."

Before he could deny it again, I leaned into him, kissing his stubbled jaw and moving to his lips. He accepted my kiss, but only for a brief moment before pulling away. I could tell he planned to leave me in our bed alone. He was putting me to bed like a child, but he was going to leave. My heart squeezed in my chest as he stood to his full height after pulling the blanket over me. I bit my lip to stop the trembling, but I couldn't keep the tears from filling my eyes.

"Jack, please don't do this," I whispered, fighting to hold back the sob that wanted to escape my chest. I needed him now more than any other time. After spending the last two months as little more than roommates that shared a bed, I couldn't take more distance from him. It felt too much like rejection all over again.

He hardly glanced my way as he seemed to firm his resolve, stepping away from the side of the bed and walking toward the door. I couldn't take it. My heart was breaking into pieces, and I wasn't sure if they'd ever be able to be put back together again.

I pushed back the covers that he had just tucked around me and got onto my knees. I would only plead with him once. If he walked away, I wouldn't forgive him. I wouldn't *trust him* anymore.

THE QUEEN OF NIGHTMARES

"Jack," I called out softly as he approached the door. He paused without turning around, his hands gripping both sides of the doorway until his knuckles turned white. I couldn't tell if he was trying to hold himself back from turning around or if he was that anxious to leave.

"I love you more than I ever could have imagined. But," I closed my eyes, knowing that my next words could destroy everything. He might never forgive me. I never wanted to see the look of hatred on his face in my direction, but I had to stand up for myself.

When I opened my eyes again, I could see he was glancing over his shoulder, his whole body tense as if readying himself for a blow. My voice was soft in the quiet room, and I could hear his ragged breathing. "If you walk out that door, I'll never forgive you. You'll be ripping my heart out. I know why you feel you need to leave, but we can't do this. We can't go back to how it's been these last couple of months." I took a deep breath as he turned around to face me, his nostrils flaring and his eyes narrowed, laser-focused on me as I begged on my knees.

"Are you threatening me, little Queen?" His tone was low, danger-ous. He clenched his hands by his sides into fists as his chest heaved.

I shook my head slowly, bringing my hands together to rest in my lap, hoping to still the trembling in them. I looked down at them, seeing the scars there. "No, Jack. I'm not threatening you. I'm making myself a promise. I can't hold on to a man who doesn't want to be held onto. I am worth more." I looked up at him with a tear trailing down my cheek. "You're the one who taught me that."

Jack made a strangled sound in the back of his throat as he watched the tear slide across the scar by the corner of my lip before finally falling over. Suddenly, he pushed away from the door and rushed over to me. Both of his large hands gripped the sides of my face as he slammed his mouth on mine. Jack's kiss was fierce and rough, stealing my breath from my lungs. I tasted the beer he'd barely had a sip from and the saltiness of my tears as his lips moved over mine.

He swallowed my gasp with a growl as I clutched tightly to his shoulders. It felt like I was being swept away by a raging storm, and I never wanted to be drowned so much in my life. I dug my fingernails into his shoulders, hoping that somehow it would be enough to hold him to me forever.

He broke away as suddenly as he had started, and my heart sank to the floor. I didn't want to live without him. He had become my whole world in such a short amount of time. I didn't want to walk away. I didn't want to say goodbye. But I would. For my self-respect. For my self-worth. For my peace of mind. I would leave and never look back.

I tried in vain to hold back my tears, blinking furiously so I wouldn't lose a single second of seeing his beautiful face before he walked away.

"You won't leave me," he snarled, his face so close we shared each other's air. He was practically panting as his chest heaved with his heavy breaths. I could see how wide his pupils were, nearly drowning out what little color could be discerned in his dark eyes. It wasn't until that moment I realized he wasn't angry. He was terrified. "You're *mine*. You told me that you were mine. You promised me."

His tone was nothing but accusatory as he growled and snarled, snapping at me like an angry beast. But, just like when we'd first met, I could see the truth that he held inside. In his eyes, I could see the scared little boy he'd once been. The little boy who needed his mother and had been let down time and time again was still there. Only, this time, it was me he was afraid was going to hurt him. My heart ached.

I cupped his jaw with both hands and leaned in even closer, trying to make him see into my heart. "I never *want* to leave you, Jack. Please. Don't make me leave you to protect myself."

He closed his eyes and growled, resting his forehead on mine. His voice was hoarse as he spoke. "I need to stop the threats against you, Sally. There are too many—one after another. I'm so scared you're going to get hurt again or worse, goddamn it. I almost lost you." He opened his eyes to glare into mine. "And then you threatened to walk away."

"Because you were walking away," I sighed, my breath fanning over his lips. "I have to know you will be here when I need you. And tonight, I needed you, but you weren't listening. I know you have priorities. I understand that the club comes first. I understand that you have a lot of responsibilities, but I just want to know you will listen to me when it's important. You can't walk away and put me last." I sucked in a shocked gasp as my head was tugged back by a handful of my hair at the base of my neck.

"You listen to me," he snarled, his anger shocking me. I hadn't seen so much anger directed at me before, not from him. "You are the only thing that is important. The club is nothing," he spit out. "Next to you, it is meaningless. I told you before, you are my whole world. Without you, there is no me. So, if you want to leave, you need to stab a dagger through my heart first because that is what it will feel like as I watch you walk away."

The fist in my hair wasn't painful, but he held me so tight I couldn't pull away if I tried. His body loomed over me as he eased his knees onto the bed beside mine. The hand in my hair tugged until my back arched, just on the verge of pain. He took my back to the mattress without letting go of his hold, and then his other hand moved to my throat in a tight grip. I could feel my pulse fluttering wildly under his thumb. Shame for my accelerated heart rate tried to surface, shame that instead of this large, violent man scaring me, I was growing wet from excitement. But he owned my body, and I had learned he would bring me nothing but pleasure when he touched me. I swallowed, then tilted my chin, giving him room to hold onto me more firmly.

He growled deep in his throat as he watched my reaction to his domination. He took my lips in a clashing of teeth and dueling tongues. My breath was taken from me as he carried me away on a tidal wave of lust and passion. I knew it would destroy both of us irreparably to be separated. I could only hold onto the deep hope that there was nothing we couldn't work out together. That there was no problem too big to overcome.

I knew it was harsh, giving him an ultimatum, but he was a stubborn man who didn't know the first thing about being in a relationship. But he'd quickly proven that he was the man I'd known he was. He was dedicated, loyal, and willing to do what it took to love me. The same as I was with him.

When black dots began to dance along the edges of my vision, Jack finally pulled back, allowing great, big, greedy gulps of air to fill my lungs. As I squirmed under him, Jack kissed along my chin, then down to my collarbone as his hand around my throat spasmed, even as the one in my hair released the tight hold.

I threw back my head as his hot mouth tightened around one of my sensitive nipples. I was hit with double the sensation as I felt the rough fingertips of his free hand skate along my neglected breast to settle over the nipple there. He pinched and pulled as I gasped at the pleasure mixed with pain.

With shock, I felt myself explode with an orgasm. Jack's rhythmic sucking on one nipple and the rolling, pinching of the other had sent an arrow of heat straight to my clit, until everything inside me tightened before expanding forcefully outward. My back bowed, and my screams echoed in the room, making my own ears ring.

I was lying, boneless, panting in a daze when Jack's smug tone had me cracking one eye open.

"We are going to be doing that again. Soon." He ran both of his palms over my breasts, the sensation soothing as much as it made me shiver with awareness of what had just happened.

I narrowed my eyes at him. I wasn't mad, but there was something about his overly self-satisfied expression that had me wanting to deny that he had anything to do with it. "I wonder if I can do it by myself." I immediately kicked myself mentally for taunting him. I knew better than to poke the beast, especially when he was still worked up from our argument.

The hand I adored collared my throat once again as he moved his face so close to mine our noses brushed against each other. "Mine."

Again, my breath was taken from me with another fierce kiss. His teeth nipped at my lips in between strokes of his tongue along mine. I melted back into the mattress, my whole body surrendering to anything and everything he was willing to do to me. By the time he was pulling back again, the self-satisfied smirk returned to his face. I was a melted puddle of bliss and willing to concede that he, indeed, was the only person alive capable of pleasuring me.

He tucked me into his still clothed body, his chest curving protectively over my back as his arms wrapped tightly around my waist. "Jack? Don't you want to…"

He shushed my sleepy murmur and kissed the back of my neck. "You rest, little Queen. It's my punishment for making you doubt me again."

My eyelids were already fluttering closed for the last time, and I didn't have the energy to argue with him. Though, I was going to make a mental note to kick his ass for saying such a ridiculous thing.

JACK

I woke up the same way I had the last two months. The emotions that flooded me were all the same, with regret and shame filling me, quickly followed by determination. What was different were all the reasons. I had screwed up in so many fucking ways. I thought I had been protecting her by making her safe physically instead of staying by her side as she healed. I thought she needed space to recover instead of being the shoulder she needed to lean on. I had absolutely no experience in any kind of relationship, least of all with a woman, though that was no excuse.

I did have a fuckload of determination to make sure she understood how much I loved her and was never going to let her go. I may fuck up, but I learned from my mistakes. I didn't know if she realized that if she somehow did manage to leave me, I would have chased her down. It didn't matter how fast or how far. She wasn't getting away from me. I wouldn't survive it. How did someone live without their heart?

I pressed a kiss to her bare shoulder, inhaling deeply to take her scent into my lungs. Everything about her had quickly become vital to me. I needed her scent, her touch, the sight of her in my vision.

With a last brush of my nose against her soft skin, I slowly slid out of the bed. I was uncomfortable in my clothing all night, but just the thought of leaving her warmth was enough to have me sucking up any discomfort I felt.

Zero stretched in the corner where his bed was situated, his front paws extended with his rear high in the air, before giving a full body shake. He sat down and thumped his tail a few times. I jerked my head toward the door, letting him know he should go outside to do his thing before I expected him back in the room, keeping watch over our girl. He jumped to his feet, gave a quiet rumble, then turned tail to run out the door.

I did my own morning routine, making sure to keep quiet so Sally would be able to sleep in as long as she needed. After changing into fresh clothes, I had the electric tea kettle on, getting the water ready for when she finally woke. I wasn't sure if her morning sickness was getting better yet or not. Yesterday morning, she hadn't run straight to the toilet, but maybe that was just because I'd distracted her. Fuck if I knew how the shit worked. I eyed the drawer where I had last stashed the book I bought from the baby store in town nearly three months ago. It was informative, but every time I cracked the pages open, it felt like I was a voyeur into a world I didn't belong.

While I plated the ginger cookies that she seemed to love for more than their anti-nausea properties, I made a phone call to the one guy I knew could get his hand on any weapon in existence. I had an idea for a very specific handgun that I thought my little Queen would appreciate.

I watched as Zero trotted into the kitchen, going straight to his water bowl. He took a few licks of his water and ate a few bites of his dry kibble before heading back down the hall with his tail held high. His chin was up as he marched back to the woman he saw as his. I'd have to grab him a big meaty bone from the butcher later to show my appreciation for his dedication. Even when I hadn't been there for her, he had stayed by her side.

I set the empty cup next to the plate of cookies and placed a tea bag inside to wait for the moment I heard her stirring awake. I hoped she would sleep longer, but there was no telling when she'd wake up, and I wanted to be ready.

I felt my phone vibrate with a message and fished it out of my pocket. I wasn't surprised at the report of more fucking around with our warehouses. I had guys on watch every minute of the day and night, as well as patrols throughout town. I'd stepped up the patrols ever since the first attack. When the message from the Boogeyman President had come through with his threats, I'd tripled them. He wanted me to hand over the club and the town in order to save my girl from his clutches? Fuck that. The whole situation was killing me inside. I would gladly sacrifice anything for my girl, but I couldn't turn over an entire town to that motherfucker, not knowing that he would have it burned to ashes within twenty-four hours. There were too many innocent people that I had sworn to protect. No matter how much I needed Sally safe, I couldn't let those who'd done nothing but help me when I'd needed it the most suffer. Sally needed to be alive and with me, but I wouldn't be handing over control of my territory.

No. The answer wasn't to sacrifice the town. The only true way to end the threat was to cut the head off the one making it. Oogie needed to die. Now that I'd finally backed Doc into a corner to become my VP, it was time to gather the club together to make a solid plan. The Boogeymen couldn't hide away forever. I wasn't going to play little boy games the way they were. Oogie thought he would wear us down by systematically attacking our resources, but all it was doing was pissing me the fuck off.

We were going to need to take the fight to him. The only way to get it done swiftly was to prepare for an all-out assault on his compound. I didn't have the benefit of insider intel the way he did. I had a mole on the inside, but I could never get one into his inner circle. What I had would have to be good enough.

When I heard the bedcovers rustling from the bedroom down the hall, I sent off one last text calling for Church later that afternoon. Then, I poured the steaming hot water into the porcelain cup before turning off the kettle. Carefully, I walked the tea and cookies to my girl.

I heard the water running in the bathroom as I set the cup on the nightstand. Instead of slipping out of the door with the mistaken thought that she needed space from me and then heading to my home office to figure out what else I could do to provide security around the compound, I reclined on the bed and waited.

It didn't take long for the door to open and Sally to appear. She was wearing a pair of short sleep shorts and one of my T-shirts, looking fuckable with her long blood-red hair hanging to her waist in waves. But I noticed the way her head was down, staring at the floor as she shuffled back into the room. She looked miserable, and it made an ache form in my chest.

"Come here, little Queen."

Her head jerked up at the sound of my voice, her eyes immediately going to where I was sitting with my back against the headboard on her side of the bed. Her eyes widened as if she were surprised to see me, and I cursed myself for putting that doubt there.

I jerked my chin. "Now."

Her feet started moving then, and within seconds, she had her knees on the bed and was crawling toward me. I could see her heavy breasts hanging through the wide neck hole of my shirt. They had become larger and rounder in the last few weeks, a testament to the baby growing in her womb. My baby. The ache that had formed in my chest at the realization she still worried about me being here for her dissipated as pride surged through me. I had done that. I knocked up my woman. I marked her from the inside.

Mine.

I tugged her arm until she fell into my lap, her lithe legs straddling me, her weight settling onto my thighs. This was where we should have been every morning since the hospital. I was a fucking asshole.

I wrapped my hand around her long hair, relishing the softness as the strands wove through my fingers. With a light tug, I had her chin up and poised exactly the way I wanted her.

"Good morning, baby," I whispered gruffly before taking her mouth with mine the way I always needed to whenever she was near. By the time I had kissed her breathless, tasting the mint from the toothpaste on her tongue, she had melted into me. All of her weight was pressing into my chest, and my cock was rock solid beneath her.

She ground her hot little pussy against my thick cock, but as much as I always wanted her, needed to feel her under my hands and have her taste on my tongue, to have my scent on her skin, and my come dripping from her pussy, she was pregnant, and I needed to take care of her. Her needs came first. Always.

I gripped her hips firmly and gently pushed her back until there was space between us. She looked at me in confusion, immediately trying to lean forward for another kiss. I placed a hand on the center of her chest to hold her in place as I chuckled. Reaching over to the night-stand with my other hand, I carefully took the cup of tea and held it out to her. She took it with a pout but immediately inhaled the sweet scent.

"Drink first," I told her, my hands tightening on her hips as she blew gently across the surface of the tea. "Then we can play."

Her smile lit up my dark fucking world as she lifted the cup to her lips and drank.

THE QUEEN OF NIGHTMARES

"I don't see why I have to learn this since I have you to protect me," I grumbled as Jack stood behind me. He held my arms in front of me, directing my stance until he was satisfied it was perfect. I felt him nuzzle the side of my neck, his scratchy day-old stubble rubbing along the sensitive skin there, sending goosebumps and a wave of desire coursing through me.

"Because you're my Queen. Every queen needs to be able to defend herself. And," he rumbled as he placed his chin on my shoulder next to my ear, "you look like my every fucking wet dream standing here holding a gun like this." He nipped my ear with his teeth and growled. "Now focus."

I gave myself a mental shake to rid the lust from my brain. *Okay, focus.* Easier said than done with the sexy man plastered against my back, holding onto me like a second skin. I let out a nervous breath as I stared down the barrel of the gun toward the two-liter bottle of soda sitting on the fence several feet away. I wasn't scared of guns, but I also had never held one before. "Right. Focus," I repeated.

We'd been practicing shooting with Jack's big black handgun for a while already, and my arms were getting tired from the weight. My strength had been getting much better in my injured arm, but it still got tired quickly. I had to use my right hand to do almost everything, and holding the gun for so long was taking a toll.

Before he would even let me hold it, we'd spent at least an hour going over safety rules until I could recite them back to him.

Don't point a gun unless you're willing to pull the trigger.

Treat every gun as a loaded weapon.

Aim for the center of a body; it makes the biggest target, and you're less likely to miss.

I let out one more slightly steadier breath and then slowly squeezed the trigger, already squinting at the loud sound I knew was coming. Before my eyes, a fountain of soda sprayed through the air like a foamy geyser as the bullet met the target. I let out a squeal of delight and amazement as I realized I had actually hit the bottle.

I spun around to Jack with a giant smile on my face. "I did it!"

He chuckled as he slipped the gun from my hand and thumbed the safety back on. *Oops. That was another one of the rules.* "You did, baby. I'm so proud of you."

He set the big black handgun on the tree stump next to us and cupped my cheeks. I looked up into his black eyes and felt as if my insides were melting at the look he was giving me. I had been such an idiot for doubting him. When I'd woken up to an empty bed, I had immediately gone back to all those days before, thinking that he had reverted back to keeping his distance from me after hearing the voicemails. Seeing him now staring at me with so much love and pride in his eyes, I knew he would never hurt me again.

I lifted on my tiptoes to place a kiss on his lips, needing him to know how much I appreciated what he was doing for me. He made a low, rumbling sound in his throat as he wrapped an arm around my lower back to hold me against him. He didn't take over the kiss; he simply held me tight against his body and allowed me to lead.

A loud, ear-piercing whistle sounded from behind us, and we broke away from each other to turn to see who it was. Jack's arms never left me as we watched Barrel strolling toward us with a huge grin on his face while carrying a small black case.

"Nice shot there, Red. Looks like I may have some competition for my title." Barrel gave me a wink, then Jack a chin lift. "Hey, Prez. Got that thing you requested." He rapped on the hard plastic case with his knuckles. His words had definitely piqued my curiosity, but luckily, I didn't have to wait long to find out what he meant.

Jack took the case with a nod of thanks as the men did a manly back pat. "You got it faster than I expected, even for you."

I tilted my head. "What does that mean?" I asked as I glanced between the two of them, confused as Barrel stood there grinning and Jack gave me a wink.

Jack set the case on the large tree stump next to his gun and popped the plastic tabs on the side. "Barrel can get his hands on just about any gun you could ask for. He's somewhat of a weapons expert, especially when it comes to guns, and can shoot better than anyone I've ever met. If he has you in his sights down the barrel of his gun, you're already dead."

"Barrel!" I gasped as the realization hit me. "That's how you got your name!" I grinned up at him and watched in fascination as his cheeks grew suspiciously pink. He reached up with one hand and ruffled his green hair in embarrassment. It seemed like the unapologetic cocky loverboy didn't take compliments well. "How did you get so good?"

He grunted. "I was a sniper in the military for a little while."

I could sense there was more to it than that, and my curiosity refused to allow the story to end there. "Only a little while?"

"Yeah. Uncle Sam and I thought it was best to end our relationship."

Jack snorted. "He punched his commanding officer in the nose when the guy found out Barrel fucked his daughter and tried to assign him to latrine duty as punishment."

I covered my mouth with my hand, not even trying to stop the giggles from erupting when Barrel turned a glare on Jack.

"Oh my god. Exactly how many times has your dick gotten you into trouble, Barrel?" I could barely get the words out through my laughter while Barrel switched his glare to me, crossed his arms over his chest, and refused to answer.

As I wiped at moisture from the corners of my eyes from all the laughing, Jack tugged me back to him, wrapping his hand loosely around my throat to growl in my ear. "No thinking about other men's cocks." I snorted, then turned so I could press a kiss to the underside of his chin, feeling the stubble there rasp against my lips.

"Trust me, the only cock I ever think about is yours." Then, a thought occurred to me. I started wondering about the others and how they got their names. "Doc's obvious, but what about Shock?"

Barrel finally laughed as Jack shook his head with a smirk. "Shock spent some time in a psychiatric hospital."

"That's awful," I said with a grimace. But it explained a lot when it came to that creepy smile. He was a nice guy and was the first to come to my rescue when I needed it the most by way of getting Jack to help me. But that smile made shivers run down my spine sometimes.

I hesitated to ask. "What about…" I was going to just forget about it, letting the question drop, but Jack answered anyway.

"There wasn't a padlock, safe, or door that Lock couldn't get into." We all got quiet after that as we remembered the man who'd been murdered. He'd been their friend for longer than I knew and was one of Jack's closest men. Hell, he'd been the Vice President of the club. I cleared my throat and poked him in the side, hoping to lighten the mood.

"We all know where *your* nickname came from." I traced a tattooed finger. "Maybe I should start calling you Bone Daddy," I snickered, though, secretly, I didn't hate the name.

Barrel laughed loudly while Jack just smirked and shook his head before sweeping me up into his arms. He held me so close to his chest that I barely had room to wiggle as he buried his head in my neck and bit me there just hard enough to make me gasp through my giggles.

"First of all, little Queen, it's a road name, not a nickname. Secondly, you can call me daddy all you want in bed while I'm giving you my bone."

I groaned in mock disgust as I playfully slapped his chest. "Oh, that was lame. Starting with the dad jokes already?" I squirmed as he nipped at my skin again in retaliation. I glanced over where Barrel was still laughing hard enough to double over, grabbing his sides.

"Holy shit, that was fucking funny." Barrel wiped at his eyes once his laughter had died down to the occasional chuckle. He pointed his finger at Jack. "His road name has nothing to do with being tatted up like a walking Halloween sideshow. Naw, his name actually comes from the fact that he enjoys filleting a man open to the bone. It's his favorite form of torture. He didn't start getting the ink done until after his uncle gave him the road name."

I stood there, slack-jawed, as the words tumbled around in my brain. I wasn't sure what to think about what it said about Jack that he could do that to someone. I knew he was cold and ruthless. I even knew that he could kill someone without losing sleep, but to slowly torture someone? I slowly turned until I could see Jack's face, his expression carefully blank. I decided right then that there was no way I would judge him.

I cleared my throat. "And here, all I got was the nickname Red. I feel cheated."

A look of relief swiftly crossed his features before he wiped it away. A small smirk toyed with the corner of Jack's mouth as he stared down at me. "Did you forget? You're much more than just Red. You're my little Queen, and the queen is the most powerful piece on the board. The king needs his queen. Without her, he is destined to fall."

JACK

I watched Sally as she lovingly wiped a microfiber cloth over the short barrel of her new Sig Sauer P238. It was a tiny little weapon that barely fit into the palm of my hand, but it was fucking powerful. All I cared about was that it did the job it was intended for. The fact that my little Queen had nearly lost her mind when she saw it for the first time was just a sweet bonus.

"Alright, baby, I think your new gun is clean," I chuckled as she glared up at me before smiling back down at the shiny purple Sig.

"But it's so pretty," she practically fucking cooed at it. I snorted.

"Alright, I'm glad you like it. But we need to head to the clubhouse. I called everyone to Church in about fifteen minutes. I don't think it's a good idea for the President to be late to his own meeting."

She gave a long, put-out sigh. I thought she was going to kiss the fucking gun for a second but seemed to refrain at the last second. Instead, she looked up at me with hopeful eyes. "Can I bring it with me?"

"I want you to take the fuckin' thing everywhere with you, but you don't have anything to carry it in yet. I'll get you a shoulder holster so you can keep it by your side. Your little sweater things will cover it."

She looked puzzled for a second before she let out a cute as fuck giggle. "Oh! You mean cardigan."

I rolled my eyes, took the small purple Sig from her hand, checked the safety out of habit, and set it on the counter. "Whatever. Let's go."

I tugged her into my body, giving her a swift kiss, then walked her to the door where her jacket was waiting. It had started snowing again since our morning shooting practice, so I held her boots out. "Sit."

"I'm not a dog. No offense, Zero," she grumbled but sat on the bench, letting me slide her boots over her tiny feet. Zero sat next to us, his tail thumping the floor.

Once I had her bundled up, I set the alarm and led her to the garage, Zero following on our heels.

"We aren't taking the bike?"

I shook my head. "Not in this weather. We won't be able to ride again for the next three months or so. Now that winter has started to really set in, it will be icy more often than not. Too dangerous for a motorcycle. Not to mention, the cold wind fucking hurts, and I don't want frostbite to take my nose off. Even wearing a balaclava can't keep the icy wind out at these temps."

As soon as we stepped into the garage, my girl's jaw dropped. Yeah, my truck was pretty fucking massive. It was all black with shiny chrome that I had the prospects keep polished whether I was going to be driving it or not. But it probably wasn't the large truck that she would need a boost to get into that had her in awe. I took in the intricately painted emblem of the Devil's Nightmare on the hood. Even I had to admire the detailed paint job.

"Wow," she breathed as she took a step forward to get a better look. "That's amazing artwork."

I grunted my agreement, then took her arm to lead her to the passenger side. "One of the town's people has a business doing custom art. They did all the brother's work on their bikes, too."

She side-eyed me. "Let me guess—you bankrolled them to get them started."

I just shrugged, not denying it. It wasn't something I talked about or advertised. I may have helped a lot of people get their businesses up and running, but it was their hard work that kept it solid. Those people were successful because of what they did and how well they did it. My only hand in it was giving them the start-up capital.

I jumped into the cab behind the wheel, double-checking to make sure Sally was buckled before starting the truck and pulling out of the garage, hitting the button to close it as soon as I was clear. Zero had already run back into the house through his dog door to get back into the warmth of the house. I glanced at the dash, noting the time. I should make the meeting. Others would arrive before I got there, but I wouldn't be late.

From the corner of my eye, I could see Sally running her hand over her belly with a thoughtful look. I reached over and took her free hand in mine, lacing our fingers together and resting our joined hands on the seat between us. I frowned at the distance, making a mental note to seat her next to me on the bench seat from now on. I didn't like that she would no longer be pressed up against me the way she was on the back of my bike. Then I thought of her growing our child in her womb. I supposed there wouldn't be any more riding for her even after winter was over. Her belly would be too large to ride, and the thought that it wouldn't be safe for the two of them and what kind of injuries it could cause if we were to get into an accident was enough to have me gripping the steering wheel so hard it creaked.

"What's wrong, little Queen? Is it the baby?" I tried to keep the anxiousness out of my tone, but I was sure it had slipped through by the way she shook her head, giving me a reassuring smile.

"Nothing's wrong. It's just… I could swear my belly feels rounder. Like, I didn't notice it earlier today. But now, sitting here, I think it might have grown."

My heart rate picked up at the thought of visible proof that she was carrying my baby. I untangled our fingers to reach over. She moved her own hand aside to allow me to run my hand over her belly. It did seem to be a little more rounded than I remember. I swallowed hard and had to clear my throat before speaking.

"I think you're right, baby."

She grinned over at me, placing her hand on top of mine. "It's starting to seem so real."

I growled. "It *is* real. That's my baby in there. I have pictures to prove it." I thought of the strip of grainy black and white photos tucked safely away in my cut pocket under the leather jacket I was wearing.

"I know that," she laughed. "It's just that actually feeling it makes it undeniable. I don't know," she shrugged a shoulder while caressing my hand that I didn't want to move yet. "I just like feeling it instead of just knowing it. Pretty soon, we'll be able to feel it move." She sounded excited at the thought. I could picture it in my mind now that she said it. I didn't know what it would feel like since I had never felt a woman's pregnant belly before, but I couldn't wait to find out. I would never admit it out loud to anyone, but it terrified as much as it excited me.

I pulled into the clubhouse parking lot, parking in the designated spot for the President along with the rows of other vehicles that bikers liked to refer to as cages. My men were going to be a bit grumpy now that it had grown far too cold to ride our bikes. It was always that way for the first few days. Once spring hit and everyone pulled their bikes out of storage, it would be the exact opposite. They would all act like little boys who'd gotten their birthday wish.

After parking, I got out and went around to the passenger side to lift Sally down. I waited, with my hands gripping her arms firmly, to make sure she had her footing on the icy gravel. "Watch your step." I eyed the rocks, wondering if I should have the lot paved. In the meantime, one of the prospects needed to salt the fucking ground. I wouldn't have my girl slipping and hurting herself.

We walked to the front door together as I eyed the ground warily. I gripped the heavy door, glad we would finally get out of the cold. "Do you want to wait in here or in my office?"

Sally looked around and smiled, spotting a few of the club girls. "I'll wait here." She lifted on her toes to kiss under my chin. Every time she did that, I got that tight feeling in my chest. Once she dropped back to her feet, I wrapped my fingers around her slender neck, feeling her steady heartbeat.

"Don't leave. I won't be long." The kiss I pressed to her lips was hard and fast before I let her go, striding away. If I didn't leave quickly, I'd be tempted to stay. I hated not having her by my side, especially with all the danger that seemed to surround her right now.

I stomped into the meeting room, my mood souring with every step I took away from my little Queen. Almost everyone was already around the table, only the spot at the head and two others empty. I eyed Doc, who was sitting back in his chair, arms crossed and glaring holes into me. I smirked.

"Hello, brother."

He flipped me off. "Fuck you, Bones."

Everyone around the table laughed at his display of irritation. We all knew that if he didn't want to be sitting in that seat, he wouldn't be. We also knew that it was long overdue. There was no better choice for the VP position than Doc. And there was no one I trusted more than him to have my back. As VP, if anything happened to me, he would be next in line to take over. He may not have been a patched member of the club all these years, but he'd been a part of it just as long as I had. The one and only thing that had held him back from making it official was the hours he had to spend at the hospital at the beginning of his career. He was still a busy doctor, but he was at the point where he wasn't captive to his job any longer. I knew he would put the club first as much as he was able.

I shrugged off my leather jacket, draping it over the back of my chair, and sat down just as the remaining brothers walked in and took their seats with a nod to the rest of the gathered club members.

"Alright, let's get this meeting started." I looked around the table with the gavel next to my fingers. "Let's talk about how we are going to annihilate the mother fucking Boogeymen once and for all."

THE QUEEN OF NIGHTMARES

"Hey, Kara!" I walked over, excited to see my friend. She looked me over from head to toe as she examined me closely.

"Hey, girl. I heard some shit happened yesterday after I left."

I nodded to the other girls with a small smile in greeting. We weren't close and had barely spoken more than polite words to each other, but they hadn't been mean. I wished I could make friends easier, but I had a hard time putting myself out there, especially with these girls. They were so beautiful, and I could never forget my scars. Even if Jack made me feel so good about myself that I often forgot about them while we were together, the self-consciousness always came roaring back as soon as I was around other people.

I shuddered at the memory of those thousands of little feet crawling over me. "Yeah, that package you dropped off had a nasty surprise in it. I ended up spending most of the day in the hospital with dozens of bug bites. Luckily, they weren't venomous. I just had to take some Benedryl for the itching."

I lifted my sleeve, where several bites were still red. Though they were smaller in size than they had been the day before, they were still slightly raised.

One of the other girls gasped in genuine shock at the sight. "I'd heard you had some kind of attack, but no one knew what it was. Are you okay?"

If I thought about them too much, I would start scratching at them again, so I quickly pulled my sleeve back down. "I am. It was pretty boring in the hospital, to be honest. Though, Jack and I did get to see the baby."

There was a chorus of exclamations. Apparently, it wasn't common knowledge that I was even pregnant. That honestly didn't surprise me. I hadn't been around long after we first found out, and then I had spent months in the house pretty much alone, with Zero and Kara for occasional visits.

"Oh my gosh! I didn't know the Prez had a baby on the way!" One of the girls gushed. "I bet the baby grows up to be just as handsome as he is." Her voice was dreamy as she got a faraway look, either imagining Jack or my baby. Either way, I felt a spark of jealousy. Both were mine.

I forced a laugh. "Yeah, I bet."

Kara eyed me knowingly. She was the one who had convinced me that other girls would want Jack even more now that he'd proven he was interested in women. She gestured with her eyes at the other women, who seemed to be looking at me with jealousy. Or maybe it was that they were sizing me up? Maybe they thought they could win Jack away from me. They had the skills, I was sure. But Jack was devoted to me, and I could tell in the truck how much he was already in love with our baby, too. No one could take that away from me.

I lifted my chin a little higher, trying to be the Queen he always called me. I was the one he'd chosen, not these women. Even though he'd been surrounded by their beauty night and day for years, it wasn't until *me* that he'd changed. It sucked for them, but for me, it was glorious being his girl.

I looked back over at Kara, giving her a smile and showing her that it didn't matter who wanted him. She was frowning but gave me a reassuring smile once she noticed me looking her way.

"You want something to drink, Sal? I can get them to pour you some ginger ale?" Kara asked as she slid off the stool she was perched on. I stepped back to allow her room to move around me, already heading to the other end of the bar where a prospect was drying glasses with a bar towel.

"Umm, sure. That would be great, thanks," I called as I stood there awkwardly. I wasn't sure if I should take a stool near one of the other girls or move over toward the couches. I remembered what I had seen a couple of nights ago and shuddered. No, thank you. I wrapped an arm around my middle. Perhaps I should just go to Jack's office. I'd be comfortable there, and I wouldn't feel like I was on display for the club girls as they carried on a conversation between themselves about how cute babies were and how they bet the Prez's baby was going to be the cutest they'd ever seen.

"Sally?"

I jerked my head in the direction of the voice to notice one of the girls smiling at me.

"I asked if you got a sonogram picture printed yesterday?" I couldn't remember her name since I hadn't worked with her much. It was Mindy or Mandy. Maybe Cindy?

"Oh, yeah, sorry. Jack kept most of them, but I did manage to keep one for myself." I reached into my small crossbody bag and pulled out my wallet. I slipped the little square picture from inside and held it to me protectively while everyone giggled, talking about how adorable it was for big, bad men to go crazy over their babies. I smiled in agreement, but inside, I was thinking, *you can't take him from me. I need him!*

"You're so lucky, Sally. You have what we all want." All the girls nodded in agreement as one of them spoke.

"Yeah. These bikers are just so much, you know!" Another gushed. "When they claim someone, they go all out. A bit caveman, I guess, but who wouldn't want to be claimed by a man who would do anything to protect you?"

I laughed awkwardly. "Yeah, Jack is pretty caveman, I suppose. But he makes sure I know that I'm all his." I reluctantly held out the piece of paper with my baby on it and watched as they all got as close as they could. They oohed and awed over the little dot in the middle that resembled a peanut. I couldn't help but smile a real smile as I watched them fawn over my son or daughter.

"I can't wait to hold him!"

"I bet it's a girl!"

"No way. There's no way a man like Bones would make anything other than a boy."

Kara walked back over to the group, holding a bubbling glass of ginger ale and a beer bottle. "Just as long as you bitches know that I get aunt privileges."

"I don't care, just as long as I can get baby snuggles," Mindy or Cindy sighed. "I should get one of these bikers to settle down so I can have a baby." She looked back up at me as I pulled the picture back, carefully tucking it away in my wallet again. "How'd you do it?"

I jerked my head up at the question, zipping up my purse and picking up my glass of ginger ale with a frown. "What did I do?"

"You got one of the Devil's Nightmares to fall in love with you."

A short blonde nodded with a sassy grin. "Not just any Nightmare, *the* Nightmare. He was so unattainable. None of us ever stood a chance. We're just curious what you did."

I took a small step back as I glanced at all their eager faces one by one. As I looked closer, I didn't see malice. Maybe a hint of jealousy, but it didn't seem to be directed at me personally. They all looked genuinely… happy for me. Maybe Kara was wrong. I didn't think these girls were trying to steal Jack from me at all.

"Uh, I didn't really do anything. I mean, the first time I saw him, I felt like, a spark. Then, I didn't really see him very much, but when he was around, he always seemed to be watching me. It wasn't until a month had passed before he even spoke to me." I laughed as I thought back. When I thought about the Jack I knew then, to the Jack I know now, I realized that he was just as confused as I was. I sort of loved that he didn't know what he was doing.

"That's super sweet. Though, I wouldn't mind having one of them just stomp up to me and throw me over his shoulder. None of that staring for a month bullshit. No offense, Sally."

I giggled. "None taken."

"I like how you think, Sherry," the little blonde nudged one of the others. "Carry me off to his cave and lay his claim as he lay his pipe."

I choked on my ginger ale, sputtering as everyone laughed at her words.

"Agreed. Anyone that claims me better have a big ass pipe, too. I've had it with tiny little pencil dicks."

"Pencil dicks aren't the problem, it's what they do with it. Some guys think just because they're hot, they don't have to work it. A hot guy can have an anaconda in his pants. If he can't make that thing do the mamba, then he's worthless. Throw him back and find an average fucker that really knows how to work those hips."

All the girls agreed with a cheer and took a big swig of their drinks, all giggling and talking excitedly about guys and their experiences. I was surprised that I found myself enjoying their company. I glanced over at Kara to see her sitting back, sipping her beer and watching everyone with a small smile. I nudged her with my elbow with a grin, glad she had been wrong. It was nice having girlfriends for once.

JACK

"I will send out the drones later tonight around three a.m. Less chance any patched member will be out, and prospects likely won't know what they are looking at. That's if I'm even noticed." Tech's tone was smug, but then, he'd earned the right to be. He could probably send out a drone at high noon during a barbeque and still go unnoticed.

I jerked my chin, giving him all the permission necessary to start getting his plan in order. The meeting had been productive. We had a working plan to take out the Boogeymen once and for all. As much as I would love to ride up guns blazing or, better yet, shoot off a few dozen rocket-propelled grenades to wipe them out, we needed to be smart and stealthy. And the first step was surveillance. But we had already lined up steps two through ten as well.

"I'll check our stash for C4 and all the fixings for bombing the buildings. Once we know what we are looking at," Rash jerked his chin in Tech's direction, "Once we have the layout, I'll draw up the compound diagram and figure out the best places for them."

I sat back, running my hand over my scruffy chin. I needed to shave so I didn't hurt my girl with it. I didn't like the thought that I could damage her delicate skin. "Sounds like we have a working plan. We'll need to call our inside guy back. Shock, get ahold of him, and tell him to make himself scarce. I don't care what excuse he comes up with. If he's not out of there by the end of the week, then it's his ass."

Shock nodded with a grim smile. "On it, Prez."

"There's one more thing we need to discuss." I glared down the table. "I just got word this morning that the doctor fucker that hurt Sally escaped prison. According to the voicemails, He escaped yesterday morning from his own doctor's appointment. The mother fucker walked out of there after killing his guards and the doctor."

Barell sighed and shook his head. "I saw what you did to his knees. There's no way he's able to walk long or far. He's going to need a cane, at the very least. I will put the information out around town to be on the lookout for a stranger with a cane, wheelchair, or crutches. Fuck!" He shook his head again. "How is Red taking the news?"

I thought about her panic attack last night. I knew the only reason she managed to get control of her emotions was because she had to deal with mine. "She's handling it. But she shouldn't need to. I don't want this fucker to get within one hundred yards of this town. Do I make myself clear?" I eyed everyone around the table.

All heads nodded their agreement, but it didn't satisfy me. Nothing would until the threat was eradicated once and for all. "He won't be going back to prison." I didn't have to clarify. He would be dead. We had an incinerator that needed feeding. "It's going to be all hands on deck for the next several days around here. If you have families, I suggest you move them onto the compound. Or send them away to stay with extended family. Hell, put them on a plane to fucking Jamaica for vacation. Somewhere warm out of this damn cold. What-ever you choose to do, make sure they are safe."

After everyone agreed and any questions they had were answered, I called an end to Church. I stood up quickly, nodding to my men and slapping Doc on the back as thanks. I appreciated that he'd finally stepped into his role, even if it was reluctantly.

"One sec, Prez," Horse called out before I could leave. I paused and stared, waiting for whatever he had to say. "That package that arrived yesterday? The one you wanted information on?"

I nodded, anger rising as the memory of what had happened to my girl all over again. I clenched my fists, ready to rip apart whoever had sent it. I didn't care who it was. "Who sent it?" I demanded, getting impatient.

He scratched his head as he looked at me. "That's the thing, Prez. It wasn't mailed. The shipping label was fake. Whoever sent it didn't mail it. It was delivered, but not by the post office."

I thought about that, my anger rising. We wouldn't have an address to trace it back to. It just got a fuck of a lot harder to find the person responsible. Even though I knew Oogie was behind it, I wanted my hands around the throat of whoever handed it over.

"Check the camera at the front gate. See who it was that delivered it. My girl said that a postal worker dropped it off. I want his face, then find the mother fucker." I didn't have to say what I wanted done with him. He would be in the processing room as soon as he was identified.

"You got it, Prez. I'll go talk to Tech now." With a chin lift, he was out the door.

I strolled down the hall, heading for the main room where I'd left my girl, needing to see her. Sounds of laughter and music greeted my ears before I'd even made it through the doorway. I stopped for a second to just take in the sight. Sally was sitting on a stool in the middle of a group of club girls. They were obviously drunk while she held a glass, sipping what I assumed was soda. It didn't stop her from enjoying herself and giggling at whatever one of the girls said, though.

I walked straight to her, interrupting their conversation and not giving a single fuck. Once I reached her, she looked up at me, her eyes sparkling with joy. I hadn't thought much about what her place in the club would be as my old lady when it came to the club girls, but it looked like she would be fine. I was proud as fuck to see she was genuinely enjoying herself and not acting like she had to hide or hold herself back.

"Little Queen."

She sighed happily, leaning into me. "Jack."

I couldn't resist taking her mouth right there in front of everyone. If they saw the President falling over his ass for a woman, then so be it. It would ensure they knew who she belonged to, so they would know to never fuck with her. "Did you enjoy your visit?" I asked against her lips when I reluctantly broke off the kiss.

She grinned up at me, then looked over my shoulder at the others. "I did. I made friends with Brittany, Cindy, Sherry, and Carla. We had a lot of fun talking about men."

I rolled my eyes. "Of course you did." I smacked her ass to get her moving. "Let's get home before the snow comes down any more than it already has."

She laughed as she slid off the stool. "It's like a mile down the road, Jack."

"I don't give a fuck. I don't want you out in the snow. Say goodbye."

She waved at the women and then hugged the blonde, who was a regular visitor to our home. Before we walked away, the girl, Kara, spoke up.

"Oh! I wanted to ask you if you wanted to go to the maze with me tomorrow. It will be a lot of fun, and the weather is supposed to be nice."

Sally perked up. "Maze?"

I was already shaking my head before Kara began to explain, but she ignored me, continuing to speak, making me turn my glare on her. The girl had balls because she pretended she didn't see me. "Yeah. You missed it when they had it running for Halloween because of your…" She trailed off and waved toward Sally's arm. "Well, they switch it up after Halloween, turning it into a haunted Christmas theme. It's a lot of fun. They serve hot chocolate and hot apple cider. The decorations are Christmassy but spooky. We should go."

I wanted to say fuck no. There was no way I would let my girl out in public with the kinds of threats after her. But I took one look at her pleading expression, making the words die on my lips. I narrowed my eyes at her.

"Please, Jack? The only time I've even been off the compound was to go to the hospital. I didn't get to have any Halloween fun, and now it's nearly Christmas. If you're with me, I know I'll be safe. Maybe some of the others can come, too?"

She looked behind me to where I knew Barrel and Doc were standing with beers in their hands, watching my girl tuck my nutsack into her purse. "Fuck," I growled. I turned to look at my men over my shoulder. "Get the fucking prospects to check the safety of the maze. I want them standing on guard while we are there." I pointed at a grinning Shock. "You fuckers are all coming with."

Sally clapped her hands. "Yay!"

I gripped the back of her neck. "You're going to pay for this, little Queen."

I felt her shiver as she swallowed and watched as her pupils dilated with lust. Fuck. A punishment wasn't meant to be a turn-on. My cock twitched at the ways I could punish her without letting her come. My favorite option was her on her knees.

"Let's go, troublemaker."

She huffed but came willingly, waving at the room.

"I'll text you the time!" Kara called out as we made it to the door. A blast of cold air swept into the room as I pulled the heavy door open. A quick glance showed the snow hadn't accumulated much since we'd been inside, and only small flurries swirled through the air. I grunted. If there wasn't much snow or ice on the ground, I wouldn't have an excuse to call off the trip tomorrow.

I helped Sally across the gravel lot and over to my truck, watching to make sure there weren't any patches of ice for her to slip on. I noted the salt dotting the lot with satisfaction. The current prospects we had seemed to be good at following orders. It was a good sign. With any luck, they'd be able to complete their probation period without any fuck ups.

I helped Sally up into the driver's side of my truck. When she started to slide all the way over, I gripped her thigh and tugged her back into the middle. "This is where you sit from now on."

She huffed but put on her seatbelt without complaint. "The girls are right. You bikers really are a bunch of cavemen."

"I'll show you caveman when I toss you over my shoulder and carry you to our room."

She grinned. "That doesn't sound too bad."

I raised an eyebrow, looking at her after I pulled out of the parking space. "No? What about when I pull your hair and stuff my fat cock down your throat, making you choke on it in apology."

She gasped, but I didn't miss the way she squirmed in her seat. "Apology for what?"

"For making me agree to this stupid fucking idea of going out in public while you're in danger."

She sighed and leaned into me. "You're right. I just thought it sounded fun. We don't have to go if you think it's too dangerous."

"It *is* fucking dangerous. But I will do everything I can to make it as safe as possible. I don't want you to feel like a prisoner in your own home."

"Thank you, Jack." She brushed a kiss on the underside of my jaw.

"You're still going to be punished," I warned, my tone low and full of threat.

Her voice was breathy when she replied. "Oh, I figured."

THE QUEEN OF NIGHTMARES

I was so excited I was practically vibrating as we headed into town. The signs indicating the maze were easy to follow. I looked out of the rear window to see Doc's SUV following close behind. He seemed to be just as reserved about the whole outing as Jack was and swore he wouldn't be leaving our sides.

Jack had mentioned the prospects had already checked the whole area for any possible threats without signs of trouble. Even so, they would be standing guard around the property just in case. I felt bad about that because, even though the sky was clear today, it was still really freaking cold.

There hadn't been any sign of Dr. Stein in or around town yet. When I called the number from the voicemail, I was told they had no further information. No one had any idea where Dr. Stein had disappeared to. It was strange to think that a man who could barely walk managed to get away in the first place. To think he was also able to evade the authorities was just unbelievable. Maybe Jack was right, and this whole thing was a really bad idea. I was about to call the whole thing off when Jack slowed down to turn into the maze parking lot.

It was almost like a carnival had come to town. There was a huge tent set up in the middle with rows of tables where people could sit and drink their hot beverages. Right next to the seating area was a long, enclosed building with a small line of people waiting to order.

As we climbed out of the truck, I could hear the music playing over loudspeakers. It was Christmas music but played on what sounded like an old pipe organ, giving it a decidedly spooky vibe. This town was nuts but in such a fun way. It was no wonder people came from miles around to enjoy what they had to offer.

We stood and waited near the truck as the others parked before making their way over to us. Jack fussed with my scarf, ensuring it was wrapped securely around my neck and sufficiently covered my ears while checking that my stocking cap was in place.

"I'm fine, Jack," I huffed as he tugged the zipper of my heavy coat up even though it was already as high as it could go. "Is this how you're going to be with your son or daughter?" I cocked an eyebrow, amused. He paused for a second before adjusting my scarf again.

"Probably. Why would I not make sure those that I love most are completely taken care of?"

My heart melted at his words. Okay, there was no arguing with that. When he put it that way, I would let him fuss over me as much as he wanted.

"Hey, Sally!" Kara called, and I turned to see her walking out from between two cars. "Glad the Prez let you out of the house finally."

I cleared my throat, uncomfortable at her words and the way her tone implied that he'd been purposely keeping me locked away. "It's too bad my injury kept me away for so long. But I'm here now!" I smiled, squeezing Jack's hand in apology, even though it wasn't my fault that Kara seemed to be in a weird mood.

"Yeah, you're here." She almost sounded unimpressed. I wanted to ask her what was up with her attitude, wondering if she was having issues with her boyfriend or something. "So let's go have some fun." She hooked her arm in mine and began leading me toward the large red tent. "Hot cocoa first, then we can go explore."

I looked over my shoulder to see Jack scowling but close on our heels, with Doc and the others following right behind him. We went straight to the first open window and ordered our drinks. I chose hot apple cider while Jack and the other bikers in our entourage ordered coffee. Kara sucked the whipped cream off her hot cocoa before blowing on it.

We stood near a tall patio heater that gave off more radiant heat than I expected it to. While glancing around, I realized there were several throughout the tent area, making it a pretty comfortable place to relax and warm up.

"This place is amazing!" I said as I took a tiny sip of my cider. It was delicious.

"You should see the place when it's set up for Halloween. Which, honestly, is all the time except for Christmas. That's the only time they switch it up a bit. But Halloween is something else. It's one of the biggest attractions for the town." Kara looked around at the grounds beyond the tent and pointed.

"The maze entrance is right there. It's about a half-mile long and a quarter-mile wide. It usually takes about an hour to make your way through it. Every year, they change the design so the locals don't memorize it."

"That's huge! I can't wait to try it out." I couldn't contain my bubbling excitement.

"That's what she said," Barrel snickered, letting out an oof when Doc elbowed him in the ribs. "Hey, man. Watch the goods. I've got a date later with a hot brunette," he said as he massaged the area.

"Yeah?" Shock asked with a grin. "Is her name Palm-ela?"

We all laughed as Barrel smirked. "Yeah, yeah. Whatever. No need for self-love when the ladies crave all this." He gestured down his body before making a crude gesture at his crotch. I groaned as he laughed uproariously.

"What are you? Twelve?"

He winked at me with a smirk. "I haven't measured, but I have it on good authority that…"

"Shut the fuck up, Barrel. My woman doesn't need to know how tiny your cock is," Jack growled, cutting off Barrel before he could go into any kind of detail.

"Anyway," Kara spoke up, putting an end to the jokes. "Over there is where they have pumpkin carving during fall. It's obviously too cold for that, so they have cookie decorating instead." She pointed to a smaller tent, which had a few children laughing as they used giant bags of colorful frosting to draw on some rather large cookies. I couldn't tell the shapes from where we were standing, but it was a fair assumption that they were probably pumpkins.

"That building is where all the locals can sell homemade goods like pies or preserves. One of the farms even has honey for sale."

"Wow. I don't think I've ever had honey that wasn't in a little plastic bear." I was impressed and excited to explore. I could also see a small play area for the kids and couldn't wait to bring my own child once they were old enough to enjoy it.

Jack draped his arm over my shoulders as I sipped at my rapidly cooling cider. "We'll get some honey before we go home."

I beamed up at him. "Yay!" My stomach did a twist when he smirked down at me and gave me a wink. God, he was just so handsome.

Kara chucked her empty cup in the closest trash can and then rubbed her gloved hands together. "Okay, there obviously isn't nearly as much to do since it's now winter and absolutely fucking cold, but I'm sure we'll be ready to call it a day by the time we make it through the maze. I can't wait for you to see all the spooky Christmas decorations inside. It's great! There will be bloody toys and Santa with an axe." She turned to me. "Are you ready?"

I gulped down the last of my apple cider, letting Jack take the paper cup from me before I could throw it away for myself. "Yep! I'm ready. Let's go."

"We go together." Jack's deep, gravelly tone was firm. "You stay with me at all times."

"Of course I will." I agreed quickly. I had made a promise, and I trusted his judgment. I already felt terrible that I had pushed to be here when he didn't think it was a good idea. Just the thought of why had me looking around nervously. Dr. Stein could be anywhere between here and California. He already knew where the town was. His only issues were traveling while trying to stay off the radar of law enforcement and his mobility. I hoped his knees were giving him hell.

Kara's expression hardened at Jack's words, and I grimaced. I really didn't want her to think that all he did was make demands of me. I knew that's what she had mostly seen of our relationship, and it made it hard to convince her he wasn't overbearing. Or an abuser. I left his side to take her arm with mine this time. I leaned closer so I could whisper low enough that only she could hear.

"He's really worried about my safety right now, that's all."

She tugged me forward and started walking toward the entrance to the maze. I glanced behind me to see Jack scowling at where Kara and I were connected. I gave him a quick smile, but it didn't seem to pacify him any. I knew he'd prefer it if I were next to him instead, but he could compromise just a little. He could protect just as well from five feet away as he could two.

We passed empty stands on our way to the maze, and I wondered what was usually there. I was excited to come back next year when everything was set up. I could imagine face painting for the kids, or vendor stalls, selling Halloween or pumpkin themed items. I only hoped all the threats were gone by then. I ran my fingers over the slight swell of my belly and smiled. Next Halloween, Jack and I would have a baby to bring.

THE QUEEN OF NIGHTMARES

We stepped up to the entrance to the maze and waited while Jack paid for everyone to enter. I held out my hand for a bright orange pumpkin shaped stamp. I was going to wait for the guys to get their stamps, too, but Kara immediately started pulling me through the first row of corn stalks. I looked back to make sure Jack stayed in sight

"Relax. Geez, we are only a fucking foot away." Kara's annoyed tone took me aback. I hadn't expected her to still be so irritated with Jack after I told her how worried he was.

"Kara, I told you. Jack's worried about my safety. There's a lot going on right now that you don't know about. He just doesn't want anything to happen to me. Especially after what happened a couple of months ago."

She blew out a heavy breath, then turned her head to glance at me quickly with a forced smile before looking back at the path in front of us. "I get it. But don't you think he goes too far? I mean, look how controlling he is."

I was already shaking my head before she finished speaking. "No. He doesn't control me, Kara. I swear he doesn't. He just… I don't know. It's a scary time right now. I think he feels like everything is out of his control. He can't stop the threats and is worried that I could be attacked at any time."

Kara stiffened, her whole body turning rigid at my words. I hurried to reassure her. "You aren't in danger by being around me, I promise. Besides, Jack made sure the whole place was as secure as possible before he let me come."

Alright, my last words probably played right into her concerns, but I didn't care. I trusted Jack. That was all that mattered. I looked back again and realized I could barely see the top of Jack's head. He was going to start getting pissed if I didn't slow down to let him catch up. Right on cue, I heard him call out, telling me to stop.

I turned to Kara to let her know we needed to slow down, but the words froze, my throat constricting until there was nothing but a strangled sound. Kara's free hand that wasn't looped through my arm had a gun pointed right at my side. Her now gloveless hand had a firm hold on the trigger. Flashbacks of the last time I was threatened with a gun had my vision going spotty, and I swayed on my feet at the sudden lightheadedness.

"Call out to him. Tell him you're fine, or I'll shoot him." This wasn't the Kara I knew and had come to care about. Her eyes were cold as they focused on me, and I knew then that she wasn't bluffing.

I swallowed back the nausea churning, threatening to come up. "I'm fine, Jack!" I called out, unable to control the shakiness. "Kara and I are just around the corner."

I could hear him curse and Doc reassuring him that the place was secure. I wished that was true, but I couldn't take my eyes off the barrel of the gun. I stumbled over a root, making Kara jerk me upright. She turned a corner and sped up her steps, dragging me along as I bit my lip to hold back a whimper.

"Please don't do this," I begged.

She didn't answer my plea, just firmed her jaw as she dragged me around another corner.

"Why?" It was all I could think. Why had she pretended to be my friend? Why had she taken so much time to get to know me? Was everything a lie? "Where are you taking me?" I guess there was another question I needed answers to.

"You wouldn't understand," she muttered, ignoring my second question completely.

"I thought you were my friend."

My whispered words made her scoff.

"I *was* your friend, Sally. I tried to convince you to leave Bones. But you just can't see how he controls you. He bruises you, for god's sake."

I shook my head. "I told you, he doesn't. I know it may look like it, but he loves me. He would never hurt me. Is that what this is all about? If we stop, we can discuss this. I can prove that Jack isn't hurting me." If she was doing this to protect me, I could forgive her, even though the method was a little extreme.

"No," she snapped, "That's not what this is about. I was trying to protect you. If you would have just left him, there wouldn't be a reason to use you as leverage against him. But you just wouldn't listen. Now, I have no choice."

I blinked back tears as her words settled on me. She pulled me further and further away, traversing the maze as if she had it memorized. I didn't know where she was leading me, but I knew it was somewhere I really didn't want to go.

"Please tell me why you are betraying me this way," I pleaded. My eyes were bouncing from the gun still pointed at my side to the trail in front of us, hoping that she wouldn't trip and accidentally shoot me in the stomach. I knew my baby would never survive that.

"Things aren't always about you," she snapped, turning to glare at me. She huffed out a breath. "I have no choice. My brother is the Boogeyman VP. He called me home from college two years ago. Once I do this last thing for them, I can go back to my own life. I never wanted to be here. I grew up in Texas with my mom, while my brother lived in the next town over with his dad. I hate this place. But as soon as I hand you over, I'm out of this frozen hell hole."

"And my life will be over," I muttered, the sense of betrayal making my heart ache.

"Don't be so dramatic," she scoffed.

"Dramatic? You think that me being offered to the Boogeyman MC on a silver platter to be violated is being dramatic?" My voice rose with my words as I stared at her, incredulous.

"Lower your voice." She hissed as she thumbed off the safety. I held out my free hand, begging her again.

"Please. Put the safety back on. I will do what you say, but please, put it back on." More visions of her tripping and me ending up dead danced in my frantic mind.

We turned another corner to see a Christmas display in an alcove decorated with tinsel and toys around the base. But someone had painted them to look like a bloody massacre had happened in the scene. I shuddered as we passed it.

"You know, Sally, I don't think I will. I don't trust you not to grow a backbone and try to fight me for it."

My heart dropped. She wasn't wrong. I had been contemplating that very thing. I knew if she managed to get me to our destination, it would be all over for me. Would it be better to fight her now and risk being shot? I wasn't sure Jack would be able to save me this time. I chanced a glance over my shoulder, but there was no sign of him. As I tried to listen, the only footsteps I could hear were Kara's and mine, along with our heavy breathing.

Our steps crunched over the frozen roots that were lying across the path periodically. For the most part, the path was clear. It was obvious it had been worn down with so many people having gone through the maze before us. There were also patches of ice and snow. Seeing the snow there in little drifts along the bases of the stalks reminded me of how cold it was outside. I was trembling from fear but also from the frostiness in the air.

After walking quite a distance, passing different twisted Christmas displays, I heard Jack faintly as he called out to me. I opened my mouth to respond, but Kara jabbed me in the side with the gun. "Don't even think about opening your mouth." I held my breath in terror.

"Please," I whispered, almost too quiet to hear. "Please be careful with that gun."

"Then shut up and do as I say," she snapped.

A tear slid down my cheek, and I wiped it away furiously with my gloved hand. "You were like a sister to me," I muttered as my heart ached. "You were the first real friend I had."

She let out a heavy sigh, and for the first time, she sounded truly sorry. "I never wanted to do this. You're a nice person. When I started talking to you, you were just another girl who worked at the bar. I liked you, Sally. But then Bones moved you into his house." She shook her head. "That's when everything changed."

I sniffled at her words. "And there's no way you will just let me go?" She scoffed. "What about Daisy?" A thought crossed my mind. "Were you in on it together?"

"I never knew her. As I said, I grew up in Texas. It doesn't surprise me, though. Oogie likes to cover as many bases as he can. He was pretty fucking pissed, though, when he found out your man killed his sister. Not that he cared about her or anything. He just hates to lose."

She pulled me to a stop at the edge of the maze. I could clearly see an empty field on the other side of the last row of stalks as she pulled her arm from mine. I wrapped both of my arms around my middle, as much for protection as comfort. She took her stocking cap off her head and stuffed it into her pocket, then straightened her blonde hair with a sigh, never taking her gun or eyes off of me.

"It's too late for that, Sally. If I didn't have to do this, I wouldn't. You have no idea how many opportunities I've had to incapacitate you and hand you over to Oogie. I could have drugged you so many times but didn't. Now, time has run out for both of us."

"I'm glad you said that, little Kara." A deep, masculine voice had both of us turning as a tall man slipped through a row of corn stalks. He was almost as tall as Jack, but he was brawnier, with a beer belly starting to form over his belt. His cut was showing through his open leather jacket, letting me know that this was the infamous Boogeyman President.

Kara straightened, one hand going to her hair to smooth it down over her breasts like I've seen her do so many times. "Oogie." Her tone was breathless as she stared up at the man who had been threatening the club for months. I glanced between the two of them as I watched him smirk and Kara smile shyly. So she was in love with the monster. So much made a little more sense now. She was hoping to impress him.

What a freaking joke. It made me want to slap her until she came to her senses.

"It's good to know you disobeyed my direct orders, little girl. I could have had my hands on Bone's woman months ago and had the town in my clutches. But you kept that from happening."

She shook her head as her smile dropped, and her eyes widened in alarm. "No, it wasn't like that—"

The gunshot rang out, cutting off her words, and I jumped as the blood spray spattered across my cheek. Kara dropped to the cold, frozen ground in the next instant. As I stared at the growing puddle of blood that turned her blonde hair dark crimson, a large hand grabbed my upper arm in a hold hard enough to bruise through the heavy jacket and layers of clothes I was wearing.

I didn't even cry out as he pulled me roughly through the corn-stalks to the field outside. It wasn't until the sound of Jack's bellow from somewhere in the maze jarred me from the shock of seeing yet another person murdered in front of me.

THE QUEEN OF NIGHTMARES

With a hard pull that I knew I only got away with due to surprise, I slid away from Oogie. I didn't even make it two feet before I was snatched roughly by my hair. That time, I did cry out as my neck jerked back, wrenching with pain.

Oogie laughed, not even attempting to hide his amusement at my weak attempt at running away. "Oh, no, love. You aren't going anywhere." He brought me closer with his tight grip to put his nose behind my ear and inhale deeply. "I'm going to have fun with you. Maybe I'll keep you for a while, hmmm?"

"Please, don't," I whimpered as I brought my hands up, grabbing his wrists to relieve some of the pressure on my scalp.

He shook me roughly, pulling several strands out with a snarl before shoving me to the ground. I landed on my hip, bracing myself from the fall with one hand, my wrist screaming with the hard impact of the icy ground.

"Grab her, throw her into the van." Oogie turned dismissively and walked away. It was then I noticed a dark van parked several feet away at the edge of the corn maze. I wondered where Jack's men were. They had said the place was secure.

A tall, skinny man with pockmarks on his face grinned down at me with stained teeth as he stood there wearing a dirty bomber jacket that had seen better days. He turned and spit, a long stream of saliva mixed with chewing tobacco hitting the ground a foot from my leg. I shuddered with disgust and tried to scoot away from the mess.

"I hope the Prez lets the rest of us have a turn with you, too. You look like fun."

"Fuck you, asshole," I hissed out the words, batting at his hands as he reached down for me. I swung my fist and managed to get him in the nose. He snarled, then spit more brown saliva on my chest, ruining the beautiful white jacket Jack had gifted me with. I gagged viciously, turning my head away from the sight. As he managed to get a hold of my arm and yanked me to my feet, I knew the nausea I had been battling since Kara had taken me was going to win.

As I swayed on my feet, I could feel the vomit rising. Before I could turn to the side, it erupted from me. All the apple cider I had just drunk, as well as my breakfast of French toast, came rushing out in a torrent all over the front of the greasy biker.

"What the fuck!" He cried out, letting me go to hold his arms wide at his sides. I fell back to the ground, heaving with tears running down my cheeks.

"What's going on over there?" Oogie demanded from the side of the van as he drew on a cigarette. Jack had stopped smoking months ago when he realized the smell made my morning sickness flare. I didn't care if he smoked; he was an adult who could do what he wanted, but Jack respected me enough to quit when he saw how uncomfortable it made me. As Oogie walked over with his lit cigarette in his hand, the smoke wafted toward me, and my stomach immediately rebelled again.

As I turned to my side to heave into the packed dirt ground next to me, the pale, sweaty-faced biker I had thrown up on started gagging.

"Oh, man," he whined as he bent over. "I don't do puke, Prez." I may have been lying there on the frozen ground, covered in blood, spit, and likely splatters of my own vomit, but I couldn't stop the grin at seeing what I had reduced this man to. As soon as he emptied his stomach on the ground with a moan, I had to quickly turn my head to avoid seeing it and heaving with my own nausea again.

"Fuck. We're gonna be here all day with this shit." Oogie stood over me, glaring daggers at my face. "Are you done?" I thought about lying, but in the end, I simply nodded my head weakly. "Good. Get your scrawny ass up and let's get going."

He reached down and once again dragged me to my feet, then over toward the van. As I got nearer to the open doors of the van, I could see a body inside. That's when I realized what had happened to Jack's men. I recognized the shaggy hair of the one lying motionless in the van, but that was all I could see through the blood covering him. I didn't know his name, but he had always been smiling.

Before Oogie could pull me close enough to toss me inside the van next to the dead prospect, heavy footsteps thundered on the other side of the corn stalks, coming closer by the second. Everyone turned in the direction of the maze. Oogie had his gun up and pointed just as Jack came storming through the stalks with rage in his eyes and a gun in his hand. Barrel and Doc followed right behind him.

Just as Oogie pulled the trigger, I shoved his arm up, making the shot go wide. With my ears ringing, I saw Jack snarl viciously and come storming toward us. I would have described him as a deadly avenging angel, but that would have been wrong. He resembled a demon more than he ever would an angel, with his black eyes and the tattoos climbing up his neck and covering his gloveless hands.

"Jack!" I cried out, so glad to see him. I took a step toward him, but once again, I was yanked back, falling into the hard body behind me. Oogie wrapped one hand around my throat, squeezing hard enough to cut off my air supply. His other hand jammed the barrel of the gun into the side of my head. My hat lay somewhere in the dirt after our first scuffle, so it hurt as the metal dug roughly into my scalp.

I whimpered with pain and terror, looking at Jack as he stood only a few feet away. He appeared ready to rip off Oogie's head with his bare hands as he eyed the gun the man had pressed against me. The greasy biker must have finally finished his vomiting because he grinned as he walked over to where we were standing by the van's open doors.

"Stupid fucker. We win!" His laugh cut off abruptly with a loud bang. Jack shifted his gun back to aim at Oogie, not even bothering to watch as the other guy fell to the ground with a thud.

Oogie sighed and shook his head. "That was my VP you just shot." His tone said he was more bothered by the inconvenience than losing his second in command.

I stared at the dead man in disbelief. "That was Kara's brother?" I mumbled.

Everyone ignored me.

"Let her go, Oogie," Jack growled, his tone low and deadly.

I could feel Oogie's chest move against my back as he chuckled. "Never gonna happen. I warned you, didn't I? I told you what was going to happen. Then I discovered that you are planning to destroy my compound. Did you really think I wouldn't find out that you sent a drone to map my territory? I have spies everywhere, *Jack.* You pushed my hand. This is really all your fault."

"I won't let you take her," Jack ground out between clenched teeth. His fingers shifted on the gun he was holding, adjusting his grip, and I knew he was itching to pull the trigger. "You're outmanned, Oogie. You can't walk away from this. But if you let her go, I'll let you leave."

The Boogeyman President threw back his head and gave a short bark of laughter, immediately bringing his eyes back to Jack. "Oh, how wrong you are." His tone went from amused to deadly serious with his words. He gave a loud, piercing whistle, making me wince. While my ears rang, I watched as Jack's expression didn't change, but his eyes went from deadly intent to dread. They darted from the left, where the maze was, then back to my face. I knew whatever he'd seen wasn't good. I had never seen Jack afraid before, but what was there scared the shit out of him. I sucked in my breath and held it, knowing that what happened next was going to be bad.

Movement from the corner of my eye had me shifting enough to try to get a look. That was when I realized Oogie hadn't come unprepared. Several members of his club had entered the scene, emerging from the maze where they had likely been waiting for the signal from Oogie.

I closed my eyes, inhaling through my nose as it stung with the sudden stark terror that swept over me. When I reopened them, I blinked rapidly to clear my vision, wanting one last look at Jack before my entire world was ripped away from me. As I tried to tell him how much I loved him with eyes, Jack's expression became filled with so much impotent rage that my heart ached for him.

"As you can see, gentlemen, you lost before you even played your first hand. The game is over. I win." He laughed again, then gestured to one of his men. "We're done here." He looked back at Jack. He pulled me backward with him as we awkwardly climbed into the back of the van. "If you ever want to see her again, you know what to do."

The body of the prospect was kicked unceremoniously out of the back of the van onto the cold, hard ground. Barrel and Doc had moved to stand next to Jack, both of them with a hand on an arm, attempting to hold Jack back. He shoved them off with a snarl and stepped forward.

"Stop!" He shouted. "Don't take her. You can't take her." His deep voice became gravelly, cracking at the end. "Take me instead."

"Prez—" Barrel spoke low next to Jack, sending me an apologetic look. I understood. Without Jack, it was almost certain that the club, as well as the town, would fall under Boogeyman rule. I was just a woman. Jack was going to need his men to remind him of that. I gave Barrel a small smile.

Jack growled. "No!" He strode forward, dropping his gun to the ground, leaving it lying there as he came forward. "You fucking take me. Not her, goddamnit."

"Jack, no!" I didn't want to be taken, and I didn't want what I knew would most assuredly happen to me. But I loved Jack more than I loved myself. It would destroy me if Oogie got a hold of him. I knew it was what Jack was thinking, too, though. Both of us were willing to sacrifice ourselves for each other. A sob broke through when I realized there was no winning this. Not for me and Jack.

"Done." Oogie shoved me forward as his men immediately swarmed Jack, taking him by the arms as one of them slammed a meaty fist into his gut. I fell to the edge of the van, barely stopping myself from tumbling over the side before one of the Boogeymen grabbed me roughly. He pulled me through the cold, congealed blood of the dead prospect and dropped me with a bone-jarring thud back onto the ground several feet from where they were punching Jack. He never fought back as he watched Doc and Barrel rush forward to grab me and pull me a safe distance away. I cried out as a particularly vicious punch knocked his head back, and blood sprayed from his mouth.

Watching them beat on Jack was one of the hardest things I had ever done, but I didn't want to lose a single minute of seeing his beautiful face. Doc tugged me into his arms, attempting to offer me comfort, but my body and mind were going numb as I watched them finally pull Jack into the back of the van as they heaved out heavy breaths. Jack was bent over, wheezing. He spit a mouthful of blood on the ground and raised his head to look at me. One of his eyes was already nearly completely swollen, and the other had blood dripping into it from a cut above his eyebrow.

As I sobbed in Doc's arms, Oogie paused at the doors he was closing. "I'll be seeing you soon, little girl," and then he winked at me. Jack roared from inside the van and rushed forward, heading for Oogie as the doors slammed closed. Muffled sounds of fighting could be heard through the walls of the van as the whole vehicle rocked back and forth. I held my breath, terrified of what was happening. Jack was outnumbered, with at least four Boogeymen in there with him. The sound of a gunshot made me jump and shriek. All sounds of the fighting ended abruptly. When the van started up and began rolling away a second later, I cried out, screaming Jack's name.

THE QUEEN OF NIGHTMARES

Doc carried me through the crowd of gawkers back to the parking lot as I sobbed uncontrollably. I ignored all of it, even when we stopped for a brief moment to speak quietly with a man who looked vaguely familiar. I didn't care about anything except for Jack. That gunshot played over and over in my mind on a horrible loop.

Once we got to the SUV, Doc shoved me up into the seat, quickly belting me in. Through my tears, I could see other Devil's Nightmares climbing into their own vehicles but turned away. When Doc slid behind the wheel, an unexpected torrent of rage came bursting out of me.

I slapped and punched as much as I could, trapped behind the restricting belt, too far gone to even think about undoing and making my assault on my would-be brother-in-law easier. I screamed and sobbed at Doc while he just held up his arms to protect his grim face. "You should have stopped him! You should have let them take me! I hate you! I hate you! Get him back!" My door opened behind me, and I felt large arms wrap around me, holding me still as I struggled to free myself as my chest heaved. "It should have been me!" I screamed, ending with a sob.

"No, Red." I recognized the voice as Barrel, and that just spurred me on. He had been there, too. He should have stopped Jack from sacrificing himself for me. That shot reverberated in my mind like a broken record, making my shoulders shake from how hard I was crying.

"I'm sorry, Sally," Doc muttered.

I felt a prick in my upper arm and glanced down through blurry eyes to see Doc pulling a syringe back. I moaned in defeat. "Jack."

"I know, Red," Barrel whispered into my hair as his grip loosened. "I know."

I slumped back into my seat. My whole body trembled even as my sobs quieted to whimpering while the tears continued to stream down my cheeks to drip off my chin. I rolled my head against the headrest. "Not Jack. Not Jack." I whispered. "It should have been me."

I felt the door close, and the vehicle start up. "Red, the town would be in ashes anyway if they had taken you. Bones would have burned down the whole fucking town in a rage." I heard Doc's words, but I didn't care. I didn't care about anything but Jack. Let the whole fucking world burn.

My eyes must have closed as we drove through the town. Once we pulled back into the compound and parked in the lot in front of the clubhouse, my door opened again. Barrel clicked my seatbelt, and I felt it loosen from around me. He lifted my arm to allow it to slide from around my body. I blinked at him, my eyelids feeling heavy.

Doc moved to his side, and Barrel stepped back, a sad expression on his face as he looked down at me. I glanced over at Doc as he reached for me. I allowed him to slide his arms under and lift me. As I stared at his profile I could see the same features that both he and Jack shared. I squeezed my eyes closed to shut out the image as a fresh wave of tears began to fall.

"I hate you," I whispered.

Doc heaved out a heavy sigh. "Not as much as I hate myself, little Red."

A few minutes later, I felt myself being lowered. I felt the familiar leather of the couch in Jack's office under me. I almost begged for him to take me anywhere else, but when he placed the throw over me, I got a whiff of Jack's scent on it and pulled it closer. Quiet sobs took over, not allowing me to say anything else.

A hand rested on my shoulder. Doc's deep voice was soft as he told me to sleep. "We're going to be in Church, Red. I swear, we are going to do everything we can to get my brother back." Without waiting for a response, he turned and strode out of the room, the door closing behind him with a soft snick.

I hiccuped as my heart ached so much it felt like my chest was literally being ripped apart. I had to rub there just to make sure I wasn't bleeding out all over the leather.

DOC

We sat around the conference table. Every patched member of the Devil's Nightmares filled the room. Every seat was taken, and a few were leaning against the walls. Several men were chain-smoking, making the air in the room hazy as we discussed the situation. Each of the men were filled with rage. We all pretended to ignore the empty chair at the head of the table.

"We have the aerial footage of the compound. I say we ride over there with every single weapon we have and blow the whole fucking compound to hell."

There were several agreements to the biker's suggestion. Fuck, I wanted to agree, too. But we had to be smart.

"We can't just ram into them like two virgins on prom night," Shock spoke quietly, a grim look on his face replacing his usual smile. He played with a knife as he kept his eyes on the table in front of him. I knew he was feeling a fuck-ton of guilt for not having stayed with us when we all went into the maze. At the time, he thought it would have been better to stay outside to keep an eye on anyone entering. Jack had agreed, no one knowing the threat lay on the opposite side.

We had been discussing this shit for what felt like fucking hours and had gotten nowhere. I was tired, emotionally and physically. Barrel sighed and pulled at his green hair. "The Boogeymen know what we were planning. We have to do something else. We have to be smart about this."

Tech had already scanned the room for bugs and found two. That fucking bitch who had played Red had likely planted them at some time. She'd been around the club for two fucking years, so there was no telling what kind of damage she had done or how much The Boogeymen knew about our club. It was no wonder they had been able to cause so much mayhem over the last few months. They knew every move we were making before we even made it. It was also clear now that she had been the one behind the delivery of the insects all along. I wished she were alive and standing in front of me right now so I could put my own bullet in her forehead.

Still, though, I looked around the table. It was a real possibility that one of the men in this room was another mole. "Does anyone have any other suggestions?" I asked, heaving out a sigh as I sat back and crossed my arms. "The longer we leave him there, the worse his chances are of survival. What about the other clubs? Didn't Bones have an agreement with them?"

"What if…" one of the guys leaning against the wall spoke up as he stared pointedly at the empty chair.

"Don't fucking say it," I growled, slamming my fist on the table in front of me.

He held up his hands as several club members turned to glare at him. "I'm just saying. We have to be realistic. There is a possibility that he's already dead. Sending the rest of us in there to retrieve a dead body will just end up killing off the rest of the club."

"He's not dead."

The quiet voice coming from the doorway had everyone turning to look at her. Sally looked gaunt with dark circles under her puffy eyes. Seeing her had me trying to swallow past the lump in my throat. My little brother was in love with this woman when he hadn't let a single other soul past his walls. A part of him was with her. I glanced down at her belly, the slightest curve to her lower abdomen visible through the T-shirt she was wearing.

The biker who had spoken before she came in scoffed in derision at her words. I took a close look at him, trying to remember anything about him, but came up blank. He was average height, maybe five foot ten, with a bit of a beer belly. He was likely in his mid-thirties. But I had no idea how long he'd been a part of the club.

"I get that you want your man back, sweetheart, but get your head out of the fucking clouds. No way is the Boogeyman President going to keep Bones alive."

Sally's expression hardened as she stepped forward. "Don't call me sweetheart." She walked right up to the man, and my whole body stiffened as I watched him clench his fists. "He's. Not. Dead."

"You can have your fucking delusional dreams all you want, but I'm not dying for anyone." His words had everyone in the room bristling with anger. A club only worked when every member cared more about the club than they did themselves. It was part of the reason I hadn't joined years ago. I knew I didn't have the time to make such a commitment.

I was about to jump to my feet when I watched in what felt like slow motion as Sally brought her hand up, the glint of steel shining under the bright light in the room. She held the blade to the man's throat as he snarled down at her. I stood slowly, along with several others, as we watched and waited. This was something Sally needed to do, but if he made a single wrong move toward her, I was going to slice his throat myself.

I watched as she lowered the blade a few inches, then sucked in a breath as she slid the knife under the name patch on his chest and began sawing.

"What the fuck are you doing, bitch?" He made to move into her, but before I could round the table to get to them, the bikers on both sides of him grabbed him by his arms. With them holding him steady, Sally continued to cut until his name patch that read Bear was hanging by a thread. She pulled back the knife, and while staring into his eyes, she used her free hand to grip the patch and pull, breaking the last of the thread and tugging it off the leather. Everyone ignored his curses as he ranted the whole time she was slicing.

"I may not be a member of this club, but even I know what it's supposed to mean to be in a brotherhood. You don't care about your President? Then you're not a part of this club either."

The man looked ready to commit murder. He looked up, glancing around at the faces looking back at him with disgust. "You all are going to let this bitch come into Church and do this shit?" His gaze settled on me.

I sat back in my chair with a grin. "Yep."

Twenty~Three

THE QUEEN OF NIGHTMARES

It took a couple of the men to drag Bear out of the door. It was easy to hear him yelling as he was dragged down the hall. There wasn't a single ounce of regret in me as I walked to the head of the table. I stared down at the empty chair for several seconds until someone cleared their throat, jarring me from the thoughts of Jack that swirled through my head.

I tossed the patch down on the table, watching as it skittered to a stop in the middle of the polished wood. Without a word, I pulled the chair out and took a seat, daring anyone to tell me I wasn't allowed to be in the room, let alone sit in the President's spot. I knew I had already crossed several lines and broken a dozen rules, but Jack had made me his Queen, and in my eyes, that gave me every right.

I looked around the room, meeting each man's gaze individually. "Does anyone else have an objection to saving Jack from the Boogey-men?" When there were no grumbles or words of dissent, I clasped my hands and placed them in front of me on the table. "Good. Now, tell me what the plan is."

I expected there to be pushback. I had no business being in this room, after all, but the men just glanced at each other as if asking, *are we really letting her do this?* Doc was the first to speak up.

"The plan is to take as many weapons as we can to the compound later tonight. One of our guys," he nodded to a tall, skinny guy with shaggy brown hair and glasses. He was wearing a patch reading Tech on his vest. "Sent out a drone the other night, mapping out all the buildings." He leaned forward and gave me a grave look. "We know where buildings are, but this won't be easy. The Boogeymen will be expecting us. We can set C4 with charges to blow up buildings. We can take a shit-ton of ammunition, but we don't know where they are keeping Bones, and we know they will be waiting for us. There will likely be a massive gunfight, and several of us could end up dead."

Doc sat back and sighed, running his hands over his face. Looking haggard, he dropped his hands and stared at me. All the pain and hopelessness he felt was easy to read. "Even if we do all that, we still may not find Bones alive."

I bit my lip to stop it from trembling. Everything he said was true. As I looked around the room, I saw looks of determination. There was a heavy dose of fear, but I could see each of these men were willing to take the chance, knowing that they could very well lose their own life by saving Jack's.

I nodded. "I understand. You can't go in guns blazing. It won't work, and Jack wouldn't want the rest of you to lose your lives to save him. Perhaps what we need to do is the unexpected."

"What do you suggest?" Shock asked, watching me with an intense expression. I could feel him trying to read me as if he could dig into my brain and find all my secrets.

"I think we need someone who is familiar with the compound. Someone who will know where Jack is being held. Someone that no one will expect."

Barrel snorted. "That includes… absolutely no one. It sounds like a great plan, but unless you know something the rest of us don't, then we are back at square one." He looked around the table. "Maybe one of us can sneak in to take a look around. If we are careful, we should be able to find where he is. We can take out whatever guards there might be quietly. Once we have him back, then we can return to Plan A and wipe the fuckers off the planet."

There were a lot of agreements around the table. Most of the guys started discussing who would be best for the job, with several volunteers ready to take the risk. As I sat there and watched, I could feel eyes on me. I looked up to see both Doc and Shock staring at me intently. I chose to ignore their probing eyes. There were questions I couldn't answer at the moment.

I stood up from Jack's chair and nodded at the two men while the rest of them continued to discuss the plan. Someone had opened a notebook and was making notes. A small bit of warmth filled me at the sight of so many of Jack's men ready to charge into danger for him. It was too small to override the aching coldness that had taken over from the moment those van doors closed, though.

I walked out of the conference room as the two bikers who had dragged Bear out were coming back in.

"Hey, Sally, watch out for that guy, okay? We gave him a warning, but assholes like that can react kinda stupid, you know?" I nodded my head, grateful for the warning.

"I understand. I will keep an eye out for trouble."

As I walked away, my shoulders sagged under the heavy weight of emotions I was battling. I had slept for a while after Doc had dosed me with whatever the sedative was in that injection, but I was still groggy, and depression threatened to pull me under. The only thing I could fight it with was determination. I wasn't going to stop until Jack was in front of me.

I entered the office then closed and locked the door behind me. I glanced around the room, taking in the simple decor. The desk was to the left, and the leather couch to the right. Behind the desk by the window was a filing cabinet with a small fake Christmas tree on top. I didn't know how long it had been there and wondered if it was Jack's doing or someone else's. I saw a small box on the floor under the window and walked over to peer inside. I had no desire for any more nasty surprises, so I pulled the knife back out of my pocket. Using the tip, I lifted the flap of the box. I relaxed, my muscles loosening and shoulders dropping once I saw it was filled with Christmas ornaments.

I set the knife on top of the filing cabinet next to the tree and reached in for the first ornament. It was a ceramic gingerbread man, made to look as if it had been decorated with frosting. It was adorable and so well made it almost looked like a real cookie. With a small smile, I hung the gingerbread man up on one of the branches before reaching back into the box for another.

It didn't take long to cover the tree since it was only about three feet tall, but it was festive and colorful, the majority of the ornaments being gingerbread men with slightly different colors. There were no lights or garland in the box, so it was a fairly basic decorated tree. But I liked it in its simplicity.

I backed up to take in the full effect of the Christmas tree until my hip hit the side of the desk, taking my attention. When I turned to look down at it, I noticed stacks of paperwork sitting there. Out of curiosity, and a feeble attempt to take my mind off things, I shuffled through the papers and realized I was looking at reports from the various businesses Jack owned in town. There was also a stack of invoices as well as written requests for all kinds of things like changing inventory and updating logos and signage. It seemed Jack did a lot more than financially back the town's people the way he'd like me to believe. Maybe he was embarrassed, or maybe he truly believed he had no hand in what the businesses did. But from what I was discovering by looking through the papers, he actively aided them in business decisions and was still paying bills for a few of them. My guess was that the money was recorded as a loan to the ones who were still getting steady on their feet. From another financial ledger, it was clear that the repayment plans on his business loans were very generous.

My pride in Jack, the man, grew as I took in what I suspected was only the tip of the iceberg when it came to the town. I picked up the pen lying next to the paperwork and started reading through the requests again from the beginning, paying closer attention. I pulled a notebook closer to me and began making notes.

As I worked in silence, my mind kept drifting to what I had said in the conference room. I knew what had to be done, and like the men of the club, I hesitated. I wanted Jack freed more than anything, but I would be putting a woman in grave danger. Did I ask her to risk her life? Did Jack have a choice? I had no doubts that the club's plan to send in a man would fail. Jack needed someone who knew exactly where he was being kept and could get him out undetected.

With a heavy dose of trepidation fueled by hope, I reached for my phone. With trembling fingers, I withdrew the piece of paper from my pocket. I didn't know why I had suddenly needed to keep it close. After getting home from the hospital, I placed it in my shirt drawer underneath a blouse I never wore. When I was getting dressed this morning, I saw it sitting there, staring at me like a bold neon sign, so I picked it up and slipped it into my pocket. Now, as I sat at Jack's desk, I typed the number into my phone.

It rang three times, and I was about to hang up when the person answered.

"Sally?"

"Hey, Daisy. Remember when you gave me your number, you said if I ever needed anything, I could call you?" I took a deep breath. "There's something I need your help with."

Twenty~Four

JACK

Everything hurt. Even my fucking eyelashes hurt as they brushed against the skin of my bruised and swollen eye socket. I kept my eyes closed as I listened to the shouts outside that had started up just a few minutes ago. The sudden commotion had drawn them outside and ended the latest fun the Boogeymen were having at my expense, so I was grateful for the distraction.

If I had to guess, one of my men, or all of them, had come in an attempt to rescue me. I cursed silently. I didn't have time to relay any orders when I had been taken, but Doc should have known that his priority should be on keeping my woman and child safe. I could die happy knowing that they would live. If the club angered Oogie, there was no doubt he would take it out on my little Queen. He'd already threatened her several times, but his final words to her had been what made me see red.

When I heard him say those words, I'd lost my shit. It wasn't until the bullet slammed through my shoulder that I slowed down, but it was the strike to my skull from behind that had put my struggles to an end. I'd woken already strung up like a fucking deer, which was pretty fucking ironic since that was the same method of torture the Devil's Nightmares employed.

Instead of hanging me by my arms, though, I was hanging by my fucking feet. My one arm was useless. I couldn't move it at all, thanks to the bullet I had taken to my shoulder. My other arm could move, but I chose to wait until I had a chance to act. If they did anything to that arm, I wouldn't have a snowball's chance in hell of getting free. My only option was to bide my time and play the good little captive until the perfect moment came. Hopefully, it will come sooner than later.

When the yelling died down, I cracked open my bloodshot eyes. After hanging for so long, I was having trouble seeing straight. Of course, that may also have something to do with the blow I'd taken to my head or one of the numerous punches they'd landed. I was hanging like a fucking piñata for them, and they were taking full advantage. I knew I had at least a couple of broken ribs, making it difficult to breathe.

There was another concern I was facing. I wasn't sure how long I'd been hanging here by my feet, but a body could only take about ten hours before it shut down. The best case scenario would be that I died from a brain hemorrhage. The worst case would be that my internal organs slowly crush my lungs until I could no longer breathe.

I blinked to clear my vision, giving my head a small shake. The first thing I saw was the puddle of blood under me. Blood was still dripping from my fingertips at a fairly steady rate. It was likely another reason I felt so goddamn woozy. The sound of the door opening caused my body to tense involuntarily, and I had to stifle my groan of pain. I wasn't going to let these mother fuckers see they had made me weak.

"Get him down and throw him in the cage." There was no mistaking the voice of Oogie. Even through the constant woosh of my heartbeat pounding through my head, I could still hear his fucking voice. I was going to make sure I killed him real fucking slow. As soon as I could move.

Rough hands grabbed and lifted me until the chain wrapped

around my legs and feet was clear of the hook in the ceiling. My body landed hard on the cold cement ground, stealing what little oxygen I had. The cement might as well have been the icy ground outside; it was so fucking cold. The place was what I would have expected from a torture room. The temperature was cold enough to make me involuntarily shiver while the heat was kept so low it barely kept the room above freezing.

I coughed and groaned, but thankful as fuck that I was no longer hanging even as I worked to stop myself from writhing on the floor with the pain. My entire body was adjusting to the sudden change of position. My ribs felt like they were being pried out of my chest with a pair of pliers, while my skin felt electrified as feeling rushed back into my fingers and toes.

Hands grabbed my chained feet and began to drag me across the room. I was pulled inside a large metal cage that looked like it was meant for a dog. If I had to guess, it was six by six by six. It would be large enough to sit comfortably, but if I were to stand, I'd have to hunch over. I also wouldn't be able to lay out straight.

The cage was welcome, though. It meant that I would be left alone. If I could rest, I could escape. I would do anything to get back to Sally. But only if I were able to kill Oogie before I left. I couldn't leave him alive, or he would just keep showing up like a fucking cockroach.

Heavy boots walked closer as the cage door was slammed, and a padlock clicked into place. "I should really just kill you and be done with it." Oogie stared down at me with triumph. It was the same look he'd been wearing ever since I'd woken up chained and bleeding. "But you have caused me so much trouble that I just can't help but want to play with you for a little while. The boys have bets going on about how long you'll last. A few of them think it could be weeks." He tilted his head as he grinned at me. "But I think you'll only make it a few more days."

He turned around and barked an order at one of the men standing by the door. "Bring him in." He turned back to me, crossing his arms over his broad chest. "Just so you know, every man that comes to my compound in an attempt to rescue you will die swiftly. Or slowly. It depends on my mood at the time." He shrugged.

The door opened, and a body was dragged inside. They pulled him over, stopping just outside the cage before dropping his arm. Oogie kicked his side, and by his lack of response, it was apparent he was already dead.

"This one came waving a white flag. Can you believe that shit?" He laughed. "Waving a white fucking flag like this was the Civil War or some such bullshit. He tried to say that your woman kicked him out of the club, and he wanted to join me." I narrowed my eyes and looked closer. The man was wearing a cut, but his name patch was missing. His face was a mess, but after blinking to clear my vision a little more, I finally recognized him as Bear. I huffed, ignoring the pain it caused. My woman had good fucking instincts. That fucker had been pushing back too much lately, and the club leaders had already voted to put him on his last fucking warning.

"I'll be watching closely for any other tactics your men try to use. You won't be able to make a dupe out of me, Jack Ellington. You will die here. The only thing that will change is whether you're still alive when I bring your old lady in. Will you still be alive when you watch me fuck her? Have you opened her ass yet? I think a sweet peach like that would have a nice tight asshole. I can't wait to make her bleed."

He turned to walk away as I seethed through my teeth. I had to grip my ribs tight with my good arm as my breathing sped up from the picture he'd painted. I wanted to rip him apart with my bare hands and my teeth in his throat. I closed my eyes, trying to get the image he'd painted out of my head as I panted shallow breaths. Before he left the small concrete building that was hardly bigger than a shed, he paused again, his hand on the metal door.

"Oh, there is one more thing," he said in a cheerful tone. I just knew that whatever he was about to say next was going to put me over the edge of sanity. And I was right.

"I know about the baby, Bones. Imagine if I let her have your spawn and raised it as my own. Your son will grow up to be just… like… me." As the door shut behind him, his laughter echoed around the room before fading away.

THE QUEEN OF NIGHTMARES

A loud commotion woke me from my fitful sleep. I was startled, sitting up with a jerk as I listened intently. It took me a minute to shake away the disorientation and realize I was on the couch in Jack's office. Late last night, Doc had brought Zero to the clubhouse along with a duffle bag holding clothes and necessities for an extended stay. The men had decided that I wouldn't be safe at the house. As much as I longed to be in the space that Jack and I had shared, one that held his touch and smell, I had to agree. I wouldn't have felt safe there, even with a guard.

I slowly stood up, glad I was wearing sweats and a long-sleeved shirt, and patted Zero's head as he whined next to my feet. "I know, boy, let's go see what's going on out there." He huffed out his agreement, and together, we walked out of the office and down the hall to the main room to see Barrel pacing back and forth with a grim expression.

He was dressed in all black, wearing what I could only assume was tactical gear. He walked over to one of the tables and began taking off a heavy looking sack from his back and setting it down.

"I couldn't get through to look around the fucking compound." He sounded pissed. More than just a failed assignment should have caused. "That fucking weasel should have been put down instead of kicked out," he seethed.

"Who?" I asked, making every head turn my way.

"Fucking Bear was there." He started pacing again, yanking at his green hair in agitation. "As I was sneaking up to the compound, ready to get to work on the plan, the fucker showed up waving a white flag and bringing every fucking member of the club outside. There were so many men and so much shouting I couldn't sneak past. I had to stay hidden where I was until the uproar had calmed down. Luckily, no one believed him when he tried to say he wanted to jump ship." Barrel sighed in defeat. "As soon as they killed him, Oogie put every single club member on guard. They surrounded the whole fucking compound."

"Bear showed up?" Doc demanded in angry shock.

Barrel snorted. "Yeah. He started shouting about Sally kicking him out of the club. He demanded to see their President so he could join them in taking us down. Instead of listening, they killed him. That fucker thought he was going to spill our secrets, but Oogie assumed he was just a mole. Killed him without hearing him out." A few of the guys chuckled.

"Good," I said, turning around to head back to the office. I was bone weary and needed to sleep. I'd been a mess of emotions since the maze, and I knew it wasn't good for the baby. Now, more than ever, I wanted to make sure my baby was safe and healthy.

As I passed through the doorway with Zero on my heels, a phone rang from behind the bar along the wall. Everyone turned to look with surprise and wariness. It was the first time I'd ever heard the phone ring. I hadn't even known the clubhouse had a landline.

Tech was the one who walked over and picked the receiver up from the cradle on the wall. "Hello?"

His back went ramrod straight as he listened to whoever was on the other end of the line. My stomach twisted when his head turned to look straight at me with a troubled expression. We all waited as he listened without saying a word. Thankfully, the call was brief, and Tech snarled out, "We'll be there."

He turned to the room and looked at Doc. "The Boogeymen are calling another meeting at The Warehouse. He wants every club to be there for an important announcement." He glanced my way briefly, darting his eyes to my face, then looking away quickly. "He wants Red to be there, too."

"Fuck no!" Doc shouted as several of the other men cursed. I stood there frozen in shock as what he was saying penetrated.

I stepped further into the room again. "Maybe he will trade Jack for me." My words were quiet, but the bikers all heard by the way their curses got louder.

Doc stormed over to me and grabbed my shoulders, giving me a short shake as I stared up at his angry expression. He glared down into my face, his mouth tight in anger. "Never going to happen, Red."

"But—"

He cut me off with another small shake. "No fucking buts. You aren't going to be a fucking sacrificial lamb to these assholes. We will get Bones back, but you aren't going to be handed over to the fucking Boogeymen. So get that thought out of your stubborn head. You got me?" His chest was heaving as he shouted at me, but he lowered his voice, speaking in a softer tone. "You have a baby to protect now. Jack would want both of you safe."

I closed my eyes to hold back my tears. I thought about my baby and nodded. "Okay, Doc." I wrapped my arms protectively around my stomach and whispered again. "Okay."

"Good."

I nodded and turned, walking away from the angry men who still ranted to each other in low, angry tones. I swiped the moisture on my cheeks away with the back of my hand and sniffled. I had to protect the life inside me. That meant I couldn't save Jack, not by offering myself in trade the way he had. I needed another way. I thought of what I'd asked Daisy to do. She was my only hope. She had to come through for me. For Jack.

I pushed the door open to the office and waited until Zero followed me in to close and lock the door. I felt safe at the clubhouse, but I couldn't stop myself from adding that extra barrier, flimsy as it was.

I lay back down on the couch and pulled the throw over me even though Doc had brought in a comforter earlier that evening. The comforter was thick and warm, but it didn't have Jack's scent on it.

I reached down to pet Zero, running my fingers through his scruff. He let out a small whine as he lay his head between his paws. "I know. You miss him as much as I do," I whispered.

I could still hear angry voices out in the common room. Sometimes, there was shouting. Most of the time, it was just a noise in the background, like the hum of angry bees. It eventually lulled me back to sleep.

As I got dressed for the meeting that would be taking place in an hour, I carefully chose my outfit. There weren't a lot of options, considering Doc had only grabbed essentials, but I kept in mind what would be happening.

Doc had informed me that everyone would be riding in on their motorcycles. Though it was bitterly cold, there was no ice on the roads, and it hadn't snowed in the last few days. Apparently, going to an official meeting at The Warehouse necessitated a show of club force. The lack of ice meant it would be safe, even if the men would have to bundle up to protect themselves from frostbite.

I decided layers were the only way to go. I put a T-shirt on first, then a sweater over that, and would wear a borrowed jacket when we left. My pants were loose denim jeans, but I wore my tightest pair of yoga pants underneath for added warmth. My pants had deep pockets and were perfect for what I had in mind.

I had never stopped thinking that if I'd only had my gun on me while in the damn maze, Kara wouldn't have been able to force me to go with her. I could have been an ally instead of a hindrance to the men when we were confronted by Oogie. Jack may not have been taken. When I saw my little purple gun in the duffle along with my clothes, I knew I would never leave the compound without it ever again.

I picked up the gun and ran my fingers over the smooth, shiny metal. The purple shone in the light, and I smiled for the first time in what seemed like years. My heart never stopped hurting, but seeing that present from Jack was a small bit of sunshine to what had turned into a drab and dreary world.

I turned the gun over to check that the safety was on before popping out the magazine. I checked the bullets the way Jack had shown me, and then I pushed it back in with the heel of my hand. I lifted the gun and looked down the barrel as I aimed. I narrowed my gaze on the gingerbread tree, focusing on only one of the cute ornaments, before lowering the gun.

With one last swipe of my fingers over the gleaming metal, I slid it into my pocket. I wasn't going to face Oogie unprepared. I may have an entire club of bikers at my back, but I was going to have the means to protect myself. I was going to make Jack proud of me.

Twenty-Six

THE QUEEN OF NIGHTMARES

The ride was worse than I had expected. By the time we pulled into the dirt parking lot, I was frozen to the bone and wondered if I'd ever be able to feel my nose or cheeks again. Or my legs. I slowly slid off the back of Jack's bike, holding on to the seat as I waited for my legs to start working again.

Doc had borrowed Jack's motorcycle for the drive out to the meeting. Apparently, he had his own bike, but it was at his home. He felt it was easier to take Jack's since it was sitting there, unused, instead of taking his out of storage. As much as I wanted to yell at him, to tell him to keep his hands off Jack's things, what he'd said made sense. Besides, when I thought about it, I knew Jack wouldn't deny his brother the use of his motorcycle. Others, perhaps, but not Doc.

I started unwrapping myself from the protective layers Doc had insisted on. I pulled the balaclava off, glad I had braided my long hair so it wouldn't be a tangled mess. The balaclava probably helped keep my nose from getting frostbite, but at the moment, it didn't feel as if it had done anything to help. Once I stuffed it into my pocket, I pulled my stocking cap down over my head and ears. Everything else could stay on. I pulled my scarf up over my chin and hunched into it. Fuck it was cold.

The lot was already full with so many motorcycles, it was awe inspiring. I knew that there were clubs in the surrounding area, and had even witnessed it from the one time I had spent at The Warehouse months ago. The lot had been full, and the inside of the building had been packed with bikers of all shapes, sizes, and ages. That night, mostly, everyone got along pretty well and seemed more like allies instead of competitors or rivals.

Looking around now, though, I couldn't help but stare. As many as I thought there had been that night, there hadn't been nearly as many as what I was seeing now. Several of the men from the other clubs were leaning on their bikes, smoking cigarettes or joints. They were talking quietly among themselves. The atmosphere seemed subdued as they huddled into their jackets, breathing warm air into their cupped hands to warm them up and stomping their feet. It was different from how I usually saw bikers act when they were together as a group. I didn't think it was all due to the frigid weather.

A couple of the men broke away from their groups and headed over. Both of them were eyeing me closely as they approached. I didn't sense any negative vibes coming from either of them. The looks they had were more curious than anything. Perhaps there was a bit of pity, too. One of them, a tall man with a thick black beard and kind blue eyes, reached out his hand to me. He was wearing a President patch, and I blinked at it in surprise before sliding my gloved hand into his bare one. I didn't know how his fingers hadn't turned blue.

"I'm really sorry about your man. Bones is a good President. I wanted to let you know, we will do anything we can to help get him back. Like him and his club, we respect our women and protect them."

"Thank you, Talon," I murmured, glancing at the stitched name below his President patch.

He winked. "Midnight Demons at your service."

The other President, just as tall but with auburn hair and a shaved face, stepped forward, shoving Talon out of the way with a beefy arm. He also held out his hand for a shake. "The Black Wolves will also be of any help." He looked over to Doc beside me and shifted, extending his hand to my would-be brother-in-law. "I hear you're the new VP. It's nice to meet you. You have big shoes to fill. Lock was one of the good ones."

I looked at the ground at his words. My guilt over his death would likely never fade.

"He was, and I do," Doc agreed.

After dropping their hands back to their sides, everyone glanced around at the gathered bikers.

"Does anyone know what this meeting is about?" Blade, the Black Wolves President asked.

Doc shook his head. "No, but I'm sure we all have our guesses."

They all nodded grimly but didn't speak the words I knew were on everyone's minds. I clenched my hands into fists and shoved them into my jacket pockets. Jack wasn't dead. I would scream it to the sky if I had to.

The sound of dozens of engines broke into the murmuring of the bikers already gathered. I watched as every man who had been relaxed, leaning against their bikes, came to attention, tossing down their cigarettes. Their hands went to the clearly displayed weapons resting on their hips. The entire assembled group fairly vibrated with tension as the Boogeymen circled the lot and then came to a stop in the empty space in front of us.

I tugged off my gloves and tucked them into my pockets as they climbed off their bikes, laughing and joking with each other as if they didn't have a care in the world. As if they weren't holding my whole world captive somewhere, doing things to him, I didn't even want to try to imagine.

I seethed with an almost overwhelming rage as I watched Oogie swing his leg over his motorcycle with a huge grin on his face. Oogie glanced around at the grim faces of everyone standing opposite him and chuckled before landing his dark, piercing gaze on me.

"Well, well, well, what do we have here, boys? The little woman herself actually came." He looked around at the Devil's Nightmares assembled around me. "I honestly didn't think you all had the balls to bring her." He looked back at me with a nasty smirk on his face. "You caused me a lot of trouble, little girl," he tsked as if chiding a small child.

He turned around with his arms outstretched, taking in the combined groups of motorcycle clubs who had come to witness whatever it was he had called this meeting for. My entire body was trembling in fear and hatred. This man had tried to take me, but Jack had stepped in, willing to fight for me, ready to die for me. And this piece of shit monster had taken him instead. I wanted Jack back.

"It's over, fellas," he bellowed. "Or," he faced the Devil's Nightmares again, "should I say, it's just beginning?" He looked over his shoulder, and all the Boogeymen raised their fists and yelled a victory yell so loud it shook the ground and made me want to cover my ears. "This town and the entire area is now Boogeyman territory." He declared his words loud and clear as soon as the cheers died down. "With this territory in my control, nothing will stop me from using the highway from here clear to Canada. My product will be on a fast track to every town, city, school, and club for thousands of miles."

Every single biker that wasn't a Boogeyman shifted nervously on his feet and eyed one another warily. Doc stepped forward with his fists clenched.

"What the fuck are you talking about?" he demanded, his jaw tight and menace lacing his tone, hatred lacing every word. "Where the fuck is our President?"

Oogie let out a guffaw so obnoxious I wanted to punch him in the face to wipe the mirth right off it. "Your President? Oh, that's funny." He wiped at his eyes, still chuckling. "Old Bones gave himself up for his old lady here. Did you really think I was going to let him walk away? That I wasn't going to put him in the ground for the disrespect he's shown me over the years?"

My body froze, my breath refusing to release from my lungs. A loud ringing began to fill my head as his words played over and over in my brain. It wasn't until Oogie pointed at me, smiled wickedly, and began chanting "Yes, yes, yes" obnoxiously that I realized that I had been repeating "No" over and over out loud.

Someone handed Oogie a bloody vest that he took in his big, meaty fists and held up for everyone to see. It clearly had patches that read

Bones and *President* on the front. It was covered in blood and what could only be a bullet hole just over the name.

"The King is dead." He dropped his hands and then tossed the leather cut in the dirt. It skittered across the rocks, dirt, and ice until it stopped just inches away from my shoes. I stared down at the vest, seeing that hole and all the blood. My stomach rolled, and I had to swallow hard several times to keep the vomit back. I shook my head slowly. I didn't want to believe what I was seeing. Not Jack. Not my Jack. The Nightmare King couldn't be gone. *No.* That was impossible.

As I stared at the vest, I could vaguely hear the words that the Boogeyman President was saying in his booming voice. Through a haze, I heard him demanding that the Nightmares clear out of his territory. Anyone that was still in town or anywhere around it by dark would be dead by morning. Including me.

But all I could focus on was that vest.

I felt the weight of that little purple gun that Jack had bought me sitting in my pocket. For hours, Jack had patiently taught me the way to use it. I learned how to load it, clean it, and how to aim for a man. He taught me never to aim a gun at a person unless I planned to kill. With that thought running through my mind, I slipped the little gun out of my pocket and lifted it while using my thumb to slide the safety off. With my left hand holding it steady, I let out a breath and placed my finger on the trigger. While everyone was arguing and cursing what Oogie was saying to the crowd, no one paid any attention to me. I gently squeezed the trigger, aiming right at the center of the chest of the man who had destroyed my life so much worse than Dr. Stein ever had.

The sound was deafening, and everyone in the big dirt lot went deadly still as I stood there and stared at the blood. I let my hands drop back down to my sides. It was amazing how something so small, almost insignificant in weight, could cause so much destruction. Jack had been right; the caliber that went in this tiny weapon was enough to kill a man with one well-placed shot.

THE QUEEN OF NIGHTMARES

Oogie looked down at his chest. He even lifted his hand and placed it over the hole that was allowing his blood to pump from his body in a steady rhythm with his heartbeat. As thick blood flowed from between his fingers, he looked back up at me and snarled. Before I could react to the promise of my death in his eyes, he fell to the ground with a heavy thud.

I leaned over and gingerly picked up Jack's vest, knowing he would want it back.

Angry shouts suddenly exploded from the Boogeymen as what had just happened finally penetrated. Someone threw themselves at me from behind, knocking me to the ground with a jarring impact. Even as I was rolled under the body, I held Jack's cut close to my chest. I lay on the cold ground, not feeling anything but the stitching of those letters that spelled out his name.

I heard a pained grunt, jarring me from my haze, and the body over me jerked. I knew immediately from the sound of the grunt that it was Doc who was covering me. I gasped as I realized he had taken a bullet meant for me, the same way Jack had protected me. I started crying then, hating myself for everything I had put these men through. Lock had lost his life for me. Jack had given himself for me. Now Doc was hurt because of me. He couldn't die, too. It was all too much. Too much pain, too much loss.

I lay there and sobbed for everything I had lost, for everything I had found. I only wanted to find a place to hide. I wanted a place to belong. In coming to Pumpkin Patch, Utah on a whim, I had found love in the Devil's Nightmares. But, I had also torn them apart.

Once the gunfire stopped and everything went blessedly quiet again, hands shifted Doc from his position over me. He was rolled over onto the frozen ground next to me, but I couldn't bring myself to look. A distant part of me was aware that I was firmly in denial, that I had locked myself away in my brain. Maybe I was suffering some kind of delusional episode, and my mind trying to protect me from the horrors of the last couple of days.

Hands lifted me from the ground as more shouts could be heard around us. As if in a tunnel, I could hear someone saying that we needed an ambulance. That was good, right? If Doc were alive, he would need a hospital, and they couldn't get him there on a motorcycle.

Hands were brushing over me, checking for injuries, I thought. Then I was gripped firmly by the shoulders and shaken roughly, a man yelling in my face. I just blinked up at him, not really recognizing who was shouting at me but knowing it was someone I trusted. Suddenly, the arms went around me and crushed me to his chest. I let out a small sob, my lips trembling as I squeezed my eyes closed until I saw stars behind my eyelids.

"Is he going to be okay?" I asked in a broken whimper.

"Doc's fine. He will be okay, Red, I promise," Barrel said with a sigh.

I nodded weakly and tucked the leather vest closer to me, holding onto it like a lifeline. "Jack's going to be okay, too," I whispered.

He shook his head at my words but didn't answer me. "Come on, Red. Let's get you home."

As Barrel led me to his motorcycle, I glanced around numbly at the carnage. There were bodies and blood everywhere. From what I could tell, they mostly seemed to be those of the Boogeymen. It appeared that once all three rival clubs targeted them at the same time, they had no hope of winning.

Home.

Barrel was taking me to an empty house. It was home, but it wouldn't be the same until Jack was back.

I held Doc's hand in mine as the machines beeped rhythmically. It was almost strange being the one comforting instead of the one in the bed.

The door opened, and quiet footsteps walked in. I didn't glance up from the grip I had on Doc's hand, but I knew who it was without needing to look. When Helen placed a hand on my shoulder, I blinked to clear my vision before looking up at her.

"Hey, Sally. Do you want anything to eat or drink?" Without saying a word, I shook my head and dropped my gaze down to my lap to stare at Jack's road name. I knew I was being rude, but I just couldn't find it in me to care.

"I'm good, Helen. Thanks." She gave my shoulder a squeeze before moving over to Doc's other side, where she looked over the many IV bags closely, even though she had done that same thing just a short time ago.

"He still hasn't woken up?" Helen turned to me with a hopeful look on her face. She looked as tired as I felt. I knew she hadn't left the hospital for long in the two days since Doc had been admitted. I shook my head and watched as her shoulders slumped. "It's okay. The body needs to heal, and sometimes, it will put itself in a kind of stasis to protect itself. He'll wake up soon. The doctor who operated on him said the damage was minimal."

I nodded, knowing all that because she'd already told it to me. But I figured it was more of a way to convince herself at that point. I appreciated the effort, anyway.

"Still no word about his brother?" she asked softly.

I squeezed my eyes closed and shook my head again. "No," I whispered brokenly.

It had been two days since the Boogeymen were all wiped out. The few that were left behind that day to guard the compound were rounded up quickly and systematically tortured for information about Jack. But not one of them said a word as they died. I didn't know what they thought they were achieving by being loyal to that monster. I had a hard time believing that Oogie was that great of a leader.

Barrel and Shock made sure I knew that they were doing everything they could to locate him, but I could tell they'd given up hope. After every inch of the compound had been searched, the club was at a loss for what to do. The only sign that Jack had been there at all was a bloody cage and chains. With their newest Vice President in the hospital fighting for his life and their President missing, Shock and Barrel were sharing the responsibility of being in charge.

I had been spending my days at Doc's bedside, not knowing what else I should do with myself. I had been calling Daisy's phone non-stop until it stopped ringing and began to go straight to voicemail. Text messages had gone unread, but I refused to think the worst. If Daisy was dead, then that meant…*no*. I bit my lip hard enough to bleed. I wasn't even going to entertain the idea.

"Okay, Sally. I'll be back again in a little bit. Don't hesitate to push the call button if there are any changes, okay?" Helen said quietly. I nodded my agreement, and she turned to leave but paused with her hand on the door handle. "Sally? Maybe you could go down to the cafeteria and get something to eat. Maybe just a hot cup of tea to soothe your nerves?"

I thought of the tea that Jack used to make me every morning, and my heart gave a painful twist in my chest. "No," I said a little too loudly, then lowered my tone. "No, thank you. I'm good for now, Helen. I appreciate your concern, though."

Helen smiled sadly and then pulled open the door to step out. The prospect at the door glanced into the room when it opened. When he saw my eyes on him, he quickly looked away, his head turning to look forward again. The last thing I saw was him pulling his phone out of his pocket to text who I knew would be Barrel with an update.

After another hour of listening to the monitors, I finally decided I had to get up. My bladder had been screaming at me for the last thirty minutes. As I headed into the ensuite bathroom, my stomach rumbled in protest of being empty for too long. I wasn't even sure what time it was, but I figured it had to be close to dinner time.

After I washed my hands, I stepped back into the room while stretching out my aching back. I held a faint glimmer of hope that Doc would have woken up in the few minutes I had been away from his side. That glimmer died a quick death once I saw absolutely nothing had changed.

I walked over to the bedside and slid a finger over Jack's President patch before whispering to Doc. "I'm going to go down to the cafeteria for a sandwich. I'll be right back, though. Okay?" I sighed when there was no response, just the continuous steady beeping of the machines he was hooked up to. I tucked Jack's cut close to Doc's side.

Opening the door had the prospect quickly straightening up in his seat and tucking his phone away.

"There's no change," I muttered, walking past him. "I'm heading to the cafeteria for a quick bite to eat." I paused. "Do you want me to grab you anything while I'm there?"

"A coffee would be great. Black, thanks." He pulled out his wallet and held out a few bills. I tried to wave him off, but he shoved the money into my hand. "I insist. And use that money to pay for your food, too."

I didn't have the energy to argue with him, so I just nodded and mumbled my thanks. I continued on to the bank of elevators and waited for one of them to arrive. Once the doors closed behind me, I leaned against the back wall of the empty elevator and watched the numbers slowly tick down.

When the doors slid back open with a ding, I moved forward, having to dodge a nurse who was in an obvious hurry. On my way to the cafeteria, I noticed the sign for the gift shop and decided to take a small detour. I hoped it could take my mind off everything horrible in my life for just a few minutes.

The shop was typical of what I had come to expect from the town of Pumpkin Patch. Grinning jack o'lanterns filled the small store.

Everything from T-shirts to glass figurines was pumpkin or Halloween themed. I shook my head as I walked around another display and stopped.

Baby items filled the corner shelves. I had found the section of the shop meant for newborn baby gifts. I reached out and stroked the soft fur of a stuffed blue rabbit. Next to the rabbit was a lamb holding a pink satin heart with the word "girl" written across it. My hands itched to pick up the stuffed animals and cradle them to my chest. Instead, I backed away from the display.

"Is there anything I can do to help you, miss?"

I jerked my head to the side to see an older woman with gray hair piled up in a bun on top of her head and reading glasses hanging from a chain around her neck. She was wearing a smock with another pumpkin on the front. I could have sworn I had seen the same one hanging by one of the shelves.

I shook my head. "No. Thank you, though. I was just looking."

The woman gave me a sympathetic look, and I turned my head away so I couldn't see it. For the first time since I left Kentucky, I suddenly missed my mom. I walked to the entrance but paused before leaving. "Have a merry Christmas," I said softly.

I heard her say just as softly, "You, too, dear."

As I headed to the cafeteria, I pulled out my phone. My finger hovered over the name on the display before I took a deep breath and touched the screen to dial.

THE QUEEN OF NIGHTMARES

I sat at the desk staring at the paperwork I knew Jack would need done. Jack's cut was sitting to the side, within easy reach. Running my fingertips over the bloodied lettering had become a habit I didn't want to break. It was comforting in a strange, perhaps even morbid way I couldn't explain.

Zero sat near my feet on the blanket from the couch. Jack's lingering scent was there, but it was beginning to fade. I knew Zero missed Jack as much as I did, so I passed the throw blanket to him, hoping it would help. I wasn't sure it did, though, by the way he would often let out a random whine.

It had been three days since Doc had been shot, and he still hadn't woken up. When I had gotten up on the couch that morning and walked to the front door of the clubhouse, expecting to be given a ride to the hospital, Barrel had stood there with his arms crossed over his chest and a determined expression on his stubborn face.

"You're not going to spend all day at the hospital today. I'll take you later for a couple of hours, but today, you're going to do literally anything else, Red."

I stared him down for several long seconds in silence, neither one of us blinking, before finally turning around to head back down the hallway. "Your roots are showing," I mumbled as I returned to the office. I ignored the gasp of outrage as I thought of the paperwork I had neglected the last couple of days. I knew exactly how to spend my day.

I walked straight to the desk. Before I sat down, I took the gun out of my pocket and placed it next to Jack's vest. Then, I rolled the chair closer and got to work.

The door opened quietly, and someone slipped inside, shutting the door behind them with a click. I internally groaned that I had forgotten to lock it behind me when I'd returned to the office after breakfast with the guys out front. I had a lot of work to do to keep Jack caught up on his businesses, and it was proving to be a great distraction. I didn't need to be disturbed by one of the well-meaning club brothers wanting to check if I was alright for the hundredth time.

It wasn't until I heard the voice that my blood ran icy cold, and dread slithered up my spine.

"Ah, finally, my patchwork doll. I have come for you, my dear. Aren't you going to greet your father?"

I jerked my head up in disbelief. "How did you get in here?" I asked in utter disbelief.

After everything that had happened recently, I had completely forgotten about Dr. Stein and the threat he had posed. Seeing him standing there now after the hell the Boogeymen had put me through was almost anticlimactic. As if he were a weak man playing at being a villain. His overly theatrical announcement made in his nasal tone almost had me rolling my eyes.

Dr. Stein smiled while leaning heavily on a cane. "You seem to forget how long I can wait in silence, my dear. My hours of standing over a body doing surgery have well prepared me for waiting for the precise moment to make my move."

"What is that supposed to mean?" I snapped, tired of his weirdly formal way of speaking and the way he always acted as if he were the most intelligent person in the room. After the long months I spent listening to his monologues about how wonderful he was, I had been ready to poke my eardrums, just so I wouldn't have to hear it anymore.

He shook his head as if he were disappointed in a particularly dense child. "I was hiding in a shed until late last night. Once everything was quiet, I snuck into the building and hid in a storage closet." He grinned, proud of himself.

I stared in disbelief. "Where did you go to the bathroom?"

"One does what one must to accomplish their goals," he said without really answering the question. I wrinkled my nose. Did that mean he went in his pants, or did he go on the floor?

Dr. Stein reached into his pocket and pulled out a black gun, pointing it at my chest. I froze and could do nothing but stare at the barrel, the small black hole taunting me. I had seen firsthand what a bullet could do to a person's chest.

"Get up, Sally," he demanded, finally deciding to do what he'd apparently been waiting hours for. In the dark. In his own shit. *Eww.* "And shut that dog up before I put a bullet in it. I won't leave him alive this time."

I glanced down at Zero, finally noticing his vicious snarls. His wickedly sharp canines were bared, and he had drool dripping from his muzzle. Zero stood by my side, his hackles raised along his back. It was an impressive show of doggy rage.

"Zero," I whispered, "sit, boy. Quiet." He immediately sat at my command, his growls easing, but his displeasure was still projected through his snarls. He likely recognized this man from what had been done to him months ago. I figured he could also sense the threat coming from Dr. Stein and wasn't going to ignore it, no matter what I said.

"Good boy," I murmured. As much as I knew Zero could handle the doctor, the man was holding a gun. I didn't want anything to happen to Jack's dog. I loved Zero with all my heart, but I also didn't want Jack to return to me only to find out his beloved pet had been killed while trying to protect me.

I was jarred out of the wayward thoughts of Jack by the hand that reached out to grip my chin. I'd been doing that a lot lately, getting lost in my thoughts and letting the world fade away around me. This time, it had gotten me in trouble. Dr. Stein had limped around the desk and was right in front of me. He brought my face up to meet his gaze, jerking it roughly. Zero gave another warning growl that would have had me cowering in fright had it been directed at me. The Doctor was more stupid than I thought.

"It's time to end this, girl."

"Yes. It is," I said with a finality that I felt deep inside. I was sick and fucking tired of others getting killed or seriously injured from trying to protect me. And I was seriously god damned tired of having a gun pointed at me. I was done with being a victim or allowing others to take the hit that was meant for me. *I was done.* With my hand curled around one of the knives that was always in Jack's desk, I lifted it swiftly and plunged it directly into Dr. Stein's shoulder, effectively making him let me go. He dropped his cane, letting it clatter to the floor as he stumbled back several steps. He held his shoulder with one hand with a pained grunt. He continued to stumble backward until he was near the window, leaning against the wall next to the filing cabinet that held the small Christmas tree.

"You fucking bitch! You're going to pay for that! I am your father! I created you! I made you what you are. It is my right to take your life away."

I shook my head as I stared at him, at the gun that was once again raised and trained on me. The man was unhinged; I already knew that. Looking at him now, though, I could see he was at the end of his tether. The very fragile, broken fibers that were barely keeping him sane were snapping at a rapid pace.

"You didn't create me, Finkle Stein. You destroyed me. A beautiful man put me back together. He made me whole again. You are nothing but a monster. You aren't my father, and I'm not your patchwork doll. I am the Queen of Nightmares."

I reached over to Jack's leather cut and withdrew the shiny purple gun, the same gun I had recently used to end the life of the man who had taken my King from me. With a steady hand, I lifted it, flipped the safety off, and aimed. Without a single moment of hesitation, I pulled the trigger.

The impact of the bullet knocked Dr. Stein back against the wall. The only indication the man gave that he knew his life was over was the brief flare of shock in his eyes before they drooped. There was a strange, macabre image of a rose that bloomed from the center of his forehead before it began to run in thick rivulets down his eyes, nose, and chin.

"That was for Lock, you piece of shit," I whispered.

His body slumped against the wall and slid to the ground as his legs crumpled underneath him. As it came to rest on the floor, I stared at the Christmas tree that was now covered in dripping red, the gingerbread ornaments splattered in crimson, somehow making them almost more festive than before.

Heavy boots thundered down the hall, and the door was flung open with so much force it bounced off the wall, making a deep dent in the plaster where it hit. I frowned at the hole, thinking how Jack wasn't going to be happy with the damage.

Several men stormed into the room, weapons raised as they took in the scene. Zero was still growling and barking, still unsettled by the entire event. I set my pretty purple gun down on the desk before placing my hand on his head to calm him. His whole body shook with pent-up rage. I knew he would have wanted to be the one to end the threat, but I just couldn't take the chance that he'd be hurt.

"What the fuck, Red? He could have killed you!" Barrel yelled as the entire contingent of Devil's Nightmares holstered their weapons and stared in disbelief at the small man who lay dead against the office wall.

"His safety was on," I mumbled. "It was about as harmless as a paperweight."

I heard someone mutter from the group, and others rumbled their agreement while giving me the side eye. "That was a good shot," one of them said.

I shrugged. "I was aiming for his chest."

Shock stepped forward with a grin on his face. "Jack would have been proud of you, Red. You did good."

I looked up at him with a blank stare. "Will be."

His usual devil-may-care grin dropped, and that familiar look of sadness that everyone seemed to be wearing lately crossed his features. "Sally…"

I turned away, not wanting to hear it again. No one believed in him, and that pissed me off. If anyone could survive the Boogeymen, it was my Jack.

THE QUEEN OF NIGHTMARES

"Can someone get the body out of the President's office? Jack's not going to want him there when he returns."

I could see the men eyeing each other warily before a couple of them stepped toward the body.

"Wait!" I called out. "Get a trash bag to cover his head and tape it closed. I don't want his blood to get all over the clubhouse." I sat back down in Jack's chair and picked up the pen I had been holding before Dr. Stein snuck into the office. I stared down at the columns of numbers, not seeing them but needing to do *something* as I waited. With my left hand, I absently ran my fingers over my slightly swelling baby bump, mentally apologizing for all of the violence our little boy had been subjected to recently.

"We searched the entire compound. Every building. He was gone." Barrel muttered at the floor as his heavy boots shifted where he stood. I ignored him. I knew they had searched for Jack after I killed Oogie. But just because they didn't find his body didn't mean he was dead. Quite the opposite.

I looked back up when I heard footsteps returning to see the office had cleared out of bikers except for Barrel and Shock. Two walked back in carrying a plastic bag and a roll of tape and quickly got to work while Jack's right-hand men sat gingerly on the couch, staring at me as if I were a bomb that might explode at any moment. I ignored them and the two guys who made quick work of securing the body and carrying it out between them. I had no idea what they would do with it, but I had no doubts that there would be no evidence that he had ever been here. I knew I would never be blamed for his death. Frankly, I couldn't care less that I had killed two men. They had both been evil and had done so many terrible things to innocent people. They deserved far worse than a bullet.

Zero suddenly jumped to his feet and started barking like mad. For the first time since Oogie had tossed Jack's bloody leather vest in the dirt at my feet, my heart began to race. Adrenaline spiked through my system, and I flew out of the chair and raced over to the window, ignoring the way the sticky wetness oozed between my toes.

I couldn't see anything through the window but the long stretch of road leading to mine and Jack's house. I spun around, nearly slipping in the blood as Zero turned and raced out the open doorway. Barrel and Shock jumped up to follow me as I raced after Zero.

"Red, wait!" I could hear Barrel calling after me, but there was no way I was stopping.

Zero was far ahead of me but was stopped by the closed main door. He was jumping against it, trying to push his way through the heavy door. I pulled it open, hard, and he flew through it like a shot, heading straight for the gate. A car was idling just outside the gate as the Nightmare manning it held a gun at the driver.

"Open the gate!" I screamed as I ran forward, ignoring the stares of the gathering crowd and the rocks that bit into the bare soles of my feet. "Open the fucking gate, *now!*" I screamed again, my throat feeling raw at the intensity of my cries.

The man looked startled, staring at me in disbelief, but ultimately, he turned and did what I said without question. Barrel and Shock caught up with me, and someone, I wasn't sure which, put a hand on my shoulder to hold me back. I turned without looking and punched whoever it was right in the jaw, making him stumble back as the car rolled forward, coming to a stop a few feet away from me.

Zero ran to the back door of the car and barked furiously. His barks intermingled with whines as he jumped and pawed at the door. Daisy jumped out of the driver's side and looked at me with tears flowing down her battered face.

"He saved me, Sal. He saved me again. I couldn't leave him there. Even if you hadn't sent me for him, I wouldn't have left him."

"Daisy," I breathed as I looked her over. Her clothes were dirty and torn. She looked as if she'd been through hell and back. I didn't want to imagine what had been done to her on her brother's compound with him knowing she had betrayed him.

"It's okay, Sally. I'm okay." She stepped back and then reached for the door behind her. I held my breath as Zero stepped back, allowing her to open the back door of the small sedan. As soon as the door was open, he charged forward, making Daisy stumble back. His barks turned to nothing but high-pitched whines as he jumped inside the car.

It wasn't until I heard a low groan coming from the back seat that my breathing sped up. Suddenly, I was breathing so fast, too fast, and the world began to spin around me. Shock ran forward to the car, looking inside. I could barely see what was happening. Tears were clouding my vision, which was already turning dark around the edges as I fought to take in enough oxygen.

"He's here! He's alive!" Shock's shouts brought everyone back to life. Every man that had been brought out to the yard because of my screaming and Zero's barking ran forward as I stood there in shock, my knees trembling until they started to collapse underneath. As I fell to my knees on the cold ground, Shock shoved the door closed again with Zero still inside.

The last thing I saw before everything around me faded was the sight of the car that Jack was in being backed through the gate and out of the compound.

JACK

"I don't understand, Prez. We searched that whole fucking compound for you for two days! You're telling me you were there the whole time?" Barrel was pacing the hospital room from end to end, relentlessly, making the headache from hell throb even worse until I finally snapped.

"Sit the fuck down," I roared, immediately regretting it as the sharp pain at the back of my skull felt like an ice pick was drilling for brain matter. I was fucking pissed that I was in this god-forsaken hospital room instead of at home. And if I had a gun handy, every single one of my men would have been nothing but puddles of blood on the floor.

They'd left my woman behind at the compound. Someone was going to pay for that. Depending on what kind of condition she was in once I caught sight of her, it might be with a bullet through the skull instead of just through the leg. Or arm. Or both.

As Barrel collapsed into the chair, he immediately began drumming his fingers. I wanted to yell at him again, but if I did, my brain could possibly start leaking from my ears.

"The shed they use for their prisoners has a pit underneath. When I managed to break out of the cage they had me in, Daisy came in," I snorted as I remembered the shock of seeing her cracking open the door I had been working on unlocking. We'd both stared in disbelief at one another. I had been angry enough at the sight of her to start reaching for her neck, ready to squeeze, until she whispered those little words that had me freezing in place.

"Sally sent me."

Disbelief had nearly overwhelmed me, but it had certainly made me stop reaching for her. She'd told me about the car she had waiting and that the entire club would leave soon for a meeting at The Warehouse. She was right; it would have been the perfect time to escape, except someone came in, immediately raising the alarm. With one loud shout, several of the Boogeymen had converged on the both of us. Oogie, himself, was the one that had beaten the shit out of Daisy. He hadn't taken it well that his own sister was trying to save me.

I had done my best to protect her from them all, knowing that if they got their hands on her, she would never survive. It had earned me a couple new bruised ribs and a few more cuts that would probably scar, but in the end, we both survived. As it was, only the fact that they had run out of time and needed to leave for the meeting saved both of us from more serious injury. I had no doubt that if Oogie had returned from that meeting alive, Daisy would have wished she were dead before he finally killed her.

"Since he was running out of time to make the meeting, Oogie decided to throw Daisy and me in the pit together until they got back." I sighed, laying my head back on the flat pillow. "They never came back though."

It was Barrel's turn to snort. Then he started laughing so hard he nearly choked. I did my best to ignore him as I wondered what the fuck was taking so long to get my little Queen here.

"You can thank Red for that shit," he finally rasped out.

I frowned, picking my head back up to look at him with a glare. "What the fuck is that supposed to mean?"

"She shot and killed Oogie right there in the middle of the meeting in front of his whole crew." He shook his head and snorted again as I stared in disbelief at the side of his face. "He tossed your cut in the dirt and said you were dead. She just fucking lost it. Cold as ice, she pulled that tiny purple gun you got her out of her pocket and shot him dead center in the chest. It was awesome, to be honest, but she started a fucking gunfight, man. We were lucky that all three clubs were there. We managed to take out every single Boogeyman in minutes. Only a few of our guys took a bullet. In the chaos, one of the Black Wolves tripped and fell over his own bike and broke his leg. Pretty sure that was the worst injury on our side of the fight."

"Sally. Killed. Oogie." I couldn't believe what I was hearing. My sweet girl killed one of the most ruthless, murdering bastards in the state.

Barrel's smile faded as I watched, his expression turning serious. "She's been a little messed up since you were taken. Fuck, you don't know yet." He sighed and shook his head before standing to his feet again and walking over to the window. "Doc took a bullet for her, Prez. He's in an ICU room. Hasn't woken up yet that I'm aware of," he looked back at me with an apologetic shrug. "Today has been a fucked up day, and no one has had a chance to check on him yet. Between that fucking doctor showing up and then you—"

"What the fucking fuck!" I roared, not even giving a shit about my aching ribs or my pounding head. I started yanking the shit off my arms, ready to get out of this fucking hospital to get to my little Queen. I couldn't go another second without seeing for myself that she was okay. "Where the fuck is Sally?" I demanded as I swung my legs over the side of the bed. "Is she alive? Why the fuck isn't she here? What are you keeping from me?"

Barrel rushed over and pressed down on my shoulders to push me back in the bed, immediately making pain explode like a mother fucking supernova from the gunshot wound in my shoulder. I clenched my jaw and panted through my teeth as I waited for the wave of dizziness and nausea to subside.

"Fuck, Prez, I'm sorry! All right? I'm sorry. She's really okay, I promise. I'm not trying to hide anything from you. You'll see for your-self as soon as Shock gets back with her. Just sit back, and I'll tell you the rest, alright?"

A nurse entered the room, ready to turn off all the screaming alarms. She scowled as soon as she saw I had pulled all that shit off me and grabbed several gauze pads from the nearby cabinet to stop the bleeding from where I'd yanked the IV out.

"Mr. Ellington—"

"Just shut off the alarms," I growled, my head swimming with pain and nausea, making me swallow. I'd be fucking pissed as hell if I threw up. There was nothing I hated more than throwing up. And with the way my ribs were aching, I'd probably want to die. "I won't get up again. Just make it stop."

I groaned and leaned back in the bed. I was done for the moment of trying to be tough. I needed a fucking break. And I needed Sally. I eyed Barrel as he backed up to the chair and huffed out a breath.

"Goddamn, between you and that woman, I've never seen a more obsessed couple in my whole fucking life."

I grunted and closed my eyes, waiting for the nurse to do her thing before we could talk freely again. She kept glaring as she got the blood pressure cuff back into place and started a new IV.

"If this happens again, I will have no choice but to restrain you to the bed, Mr. Ellington."

"It won't." I met her glare for glare until she finally huffed, turned on her ugly, sensible hospital shoes, and walked out the door. I turned back to Barrel and waited impatiently.

"Well?"

He sighed dramatically before resting his elbows on his knees and holding his head in his hands. "She's been walking around like a zombie. We've all been encouraging her to eat, but I'm not sure how much she's actually put in her mouth. She's been insisting for days that you were alive, no matter what anyone said. Then, when Oogie said you were dead, it was like the light went out, but her determination became even stronger all at the same time. She has been worrying the fuck out of us. She spent the last couple of days here at the hospital, refusing to leave Doc's side." He sat back in the chair and looked up at the ceiling. "Until today. We insisted she stay at the compound and get some rest instead of sitting in that chair all day, you know? But then, I guess the doctor snuck onto the property somehow."

I narrowed my eyes at him, the heart rate monitor attached to my finger picking up the increased speed as my anger started to boil over again. "How the *fuck* did a stranger sneak onto the compound and make it into the motherfucking clubhouse, Barrel?" My tone was deadly.

Barrel rubbed the back of his neck. "Tech is looking into it, Prez. But right now, the answer is we just don't know."

"So what happened when the asshole broke in?"

"Red happened. Shot the fucker right between his eyes. There's, uh, actually a bit of a mess in your office. She was working on your invoices or some shit since you've been gone."

I closed my eyes and rested my head back against the pillow. I'd heard enough. I needed to see my brother, and I would get someone to take me to him soon. But I had to lay eyes on my woman before I could even think about anything else. Somehow, my sweet, pregnant woman had saved the fucking club, town, herself, and me all in a matter of days. But at what cost to herself?

THE QUEEN OF NIGHTMARES

A rhythmic beeping was the first thing I heard as I was pulled slowly from sleep. I tried to rub my nose, but a small, sharp pain had me hissing. I cracked open my eyes to look at my hand, seeing the tube taped there. I followed the tube until my gaze landed on the IV hanging from a metal pole. I glanced around, realizing with groggy resignation that I was in yet another hospital room. Only, there was something different this time.

I glanced down at my waist, where I could feel a hand resting on my bare belly underneath the hospital-issued cotton gown. My whole body froze as I took stock of what else I was feeling.

A large body was tucked in close to my back, spooning me from behind. Warm breath tickled the fine hairs at the nape of my neck. And a long, hairy leg was tangled in mine.

"Jack," I breathed, not daring to believe it was true. Tears immediately filled my eyes and began to fall, soaking the pillow under my face as my shoulders shook. I tried to hold the sobs back, but so many overwhelming feelings flooded in too quickly. It was impossible to stop.

"Shhh…" The hand over my belly lightly caressed me there. "I'm here, little Queen. Everything is going to be alright now." He continued to caress me as he brushed soft kisses against the back of my neck, just holding me as my body and mind purged the pain, anguish, terror, worry, and anger in great, big, wracking sobs. He spoke softly next to my ear, his deep, gravelly voice soothing my raw nerves.

"You did so good while I was gone, little Queen. You saved me. You saved the town. You were so strong, but you can relax now." He clenched me tighter to him as he paused before placing a tender kiss below my ear. "You are more than I could have ever dreamed of in a woman. You are more than just my equal. You are better than I could ever be. I love you, Sally. With my entire being, I love you."

As he spoke quietly, pieces of the jagged edges inside me smoothed out. Some of the pieces fit back together perfectly. Some of the pieces would always remain broken. But at least they weren't sharp anymore. Too much had happened in the last year for me to ever be the same as I was.

I had been held captive and tortured.

I had fallen in love.

I had watched the father of my child taken by his enemy without knowing if I'd ever see him alive again.

I had been told the love of my life was dead.

I had killed not one, but *two* men.

No, I would never be the same. In some ways, I was better. I had found the woman I was meant to be. I had found strength I didn't know I could possess. Maybe I was crying, but that's okay. Crying didn't mean weakness. Crying just meant that my emotions were so big, they needed a little release. Besides, wasn't it okay to be weak every once in a while?

My heart was twisting in my chest for the first time in days, not in fear or pain, but in happiness. Jack was here, he was alive, he was *holding me.* I shifted, turning to my back slowly, needing to see his face.

I had to swallow past the sudden lump in my throat as I blinked away a fresh round of tears. I would not cry. He was alive, and he was here. That was a cause for joy. So he looked a bit worse for wear, but that was okay. He would heal.

I raised my hand, heedless of the tube attached to it, and gently touched his battered face. Both of his eyes were swollen and bloodshot. It was so swollen I could tell he could barely see from one of them, if at all. Multiple areas had been either taped or sewn on his eyebrows, cheeks bone, the bridge of his nose, and upper lip.

He pressed harder into my hand. Instinct told me to pull away so I wouldn't cause him pain, but I held still, allowing him to choose how much touch he could handle.

"Jack." His name was hardly more than a whisper, I wasn't even sure if it made it past my lips, but he knew I said it.

Jack leaned down and softly pressed his lips to mine in a sweet caress. I could feel the intensity of his gaze as he leaned back to peer at me through his one good eye. "You are the most beautiful thing I've ever seen, little Queen."

He tried to lift his hand to touch me the way I was touching him, but our IV lines got caught together. I choked out a watery laugh as we pulled apart.

"You should rest more, baby. The doctor said you were suffering from exhaustion and dehydration." I only sighed and carefully returned to the position I had woken up in. I had no idea how long I'd been asleep in his arms, but now that he was with me, I felt as if I could sleep for days, finally able to truly relax and rest.

I yawned as I settled in. "How are they letting us stay in the same bed?" I murmured, not caring. I loved it, but I knew it went against policy.

"It was either this," he grumbled as he tightened his arm around me, "or I walked out of here without treatment."

I hummed. I knew there was more to the story, but I doubted he would elaborate. "Will you tell me what happened while you were there?" I asked sleepily.

"Not now," he said, kissing the top of my head. "Maybe if you get some rest, and after the doctor says you're back to full strength." I pouted with my eyes closed. I'd say I could handle it, but I knew there would be no arguing with him. "And, little Queen?"

I tensed at his suddenly serious tone. "Yes?" My eyes popped open to stare at the window across the room.

"Once we are both back home, I'm going to punish you for not taking care of yourself better." I swallowed hard, not liking what that would mean, but also, Jack was alive and capable of punishing me. So, as I drifted off to sleep, it was with a smile on my face.

A door banging open startled me awake, nearly making me bolt upright in the unfamiliar bed I was lying in. Only the heavy arm wrapped across my middle kept me in place.

"Shit, Prez, I'm sorry." The sound of Barrel's gruff voice coming from the other side of the room had me settling again, my heart rate slowing back to its normal rhythm. "But I thought you'd like to know that Doc just woke up."

I gasped, trying to sit up again, but Jack gently pushed me right back down. His tone was calm, though I could hear the urgency he was trying to hide. "Good. Let the nurse know that we want to go see him as soon as they are done looking him over." Barrel jerked his chin and immediately left to do what Jack had ordered.

Once the door closed, much softer than it had been opened, I turned over the way I had the last time I had woken. Jack was already looking down at me. I could see that I didn't have to tell him, but the words slipped out anyway through my tight throat.

"He took a bullet for me, Jack. I'm so sorry. He covered me with his body. It's all my fault."

"He did what any man in the club would do, little Queen."

I shook my head. "No. It's my fault that they were even shooting. I started it by shooting Oogie and killing him." I closed my eyes, remembering the scene. The way the blood had poured from his chest as everyone stood in stunned disbelief. "I just didn't think about what I was doing. He tossed your cut in the dirt, and suddenly, my gun was in my hand. I just…pulled the trigger, and then he was on the ground."

"You thought I was dead." He said softly in the deep, gravelly voice I loved. I shook my head.

"No. I knew you weren't dead. I tried to tell everyone, but no one believed me. They were walking around, sad and angry. I just wanted you back." I blinked up at him. "They said they searched the whole compound, but the only sign of you alive was an empty cage. Where were you? How did Daisy find you?"

He huffed out a breath. "That's something else we are going to need to talk about." He kissed the tip of my nose. "Later. But to appease your curiosity, there was a pit under the room where the cage was. There was a trap door hidden in the floor. Daisy and I were thrown in there before they left for the meeting."

I gasped in horror. "You were in a hole in the floor for two days? How did you escape?" Then I thought of something else. "Did you have any food or water?"

He grimaced. "Unfortunately, they left us with nothing before heading out to the meeting with the other clubs. I don't know if they would have given us food or water once they returned, but," he lifted his arm, indicating the IV fluids. "This is the first drink I've had since that shitty coffee at the maze."

I scowled. "That's not funny, Jack. How did you get out?"

He sighed and ran his hand over my hair carefully so as to not pull either one of our IV lines. "Daisy was unconscious for an entire day with a bit of a head injury." He didn't elaborate, but I could just imagine what had happened to her after seeing her appearance at the compound. "Once she came to, I had to lift her up to push the hatch open. We're just really fucking lucky it wasn't bolted shut. I guess they hadn't thought anyone could escape."

"You lifted her?" I asked as I looked him over, noticing the way his arm was bandaged and the stiff way he held his torso.

"I had to get back to you."

THE QUEEN OF NIGHTMARES

The nurse wasn't happy when she came into the room. She scowled the entire time she separated our lines. I was incredibly grateful when Helen came in a few minutes later with a huge smile on her face and an announcement that my IV could come out.

Once I was freed, I put my own clothes back on, then sat back in a chair to watch as Jack was fussed over. He growled when he was informed that he would have to ride in a wheelchair or he wasn't leaving the bed at all. He only gave in when I promised I would ride in his lap. That earned both of us another glare, but neither one of us cared.

Once he was situated, I carefully climbed up onto his lap. I attempted to keep most of my weight on his thighs and off his chest, but with a heavy hand to my middle, he pulled me snugly against him, all while ignoring the shrill protests of the nurse. She finally huffed out an angry retort and stomped out of the room. As she passed Helen, she told her she didn't want to have anything to do with us and that she could take over. Everyone breathed a little easier after that.

Helen was all smiles as we passed the patched member who had been standing guard at the door. As she wheeled us down the corridor and to the elevator, I glanced back to see the biker following us closely with a clearly relieved expression.

After a short elevator ride to the next floor, we got off, Helen easily pushing the wheelchair with our combined weight in it. I knew she had to be as excited that Doc was awake as we were. If Doc didn't pull his head out of his ass and ask Helen out on a date soon, I was going to kick his ass.

I didn't have to guess which room Doc was in since there was another patched member standing at the door with his arms crossed. When he saw us, he dropped his arms and stared at Jack as if he thought he'd never see him again. There was disbelief, relief, and regret written all over his features. He stepped forward to meet us.

"She swore you were alive, Prez." He shook his head. "We should have known. A bastard like you wouldn't die that easy." He held out his hand, and Jack took it in a firm hold. "Glad to have you back, Prez."

I smiled but pretended not to see the glassy sheen to the biker's eyes as Jack grunted a response. He stepped back and reached for Doc's door, holding it open for Helen to push us through.

I heard the beeping machines right away, but Doc's pale, tired face was the first thing I saw. When he turned his head and saw Jack sitting there, alive, for the first time, a smile curved his lips, and his eyes lit up. I slowly slid from Jack's lap, careful not to jostle him, ignoring his reaching hand.

"Get back here."

I ignored his growl and stepped back, keeping my head down.

"Red." Doc's soft voice had me reluctantly leaving my examination of the tiled floor. I hesitantly glanced up at Doc. "Get over here." Jack sighed but didn't argue.

With a stifled sob, I stepped toward Doc's outstretched arms and carefully wrapped my arms around him. "I'm so sorry."

"Don't ever be sorry, Red. You're my sister. I would die for you." Doc's words were soft as he spoke into my hair. I breathed out a ragged breath, so grateful that he was alive.

Jack was wheeled forward until he was right up against the side of the bed so he could reach out his good hand to his brother as I straightened back up. "Thank you," he said as they grasped hands firmly.

He and Doc stared at each other for a long minute, communicating something between them that wasn't for anyone else. My heart ached with warmth and gratitude that my little family was whole again. Everyone had made it through this nightmare. We were all a mess, some of us more than others, but we were alive.

I stepped back so the brothers could have a quiet moment to talk without an audience. I moved over to Helen's side and did something Jack had forbidden me to do.

"Don't give up on him, Helen. If you care about him, make him see it. He needs a good woman by his side."

She blinked at me with a hopeful smile. "You think I can be that woman for him?"

"I think you're the only one who can." I wrapped an arm around her waist and gave her a small, one-armed hug. "What do you think about dogs?"

Her giggle had both men turning to look at us. Jack had a narrowed-eyed look as he took in our close positions, but a smile teased the corner of his mouth. Doc's expression turned soft and warm when he looked over the nurse. Yeah, they would be just fine. A little bit of pushing never hurt anyone.

We stayed in Doc's room, talking and laughing quietly until it was obvious that Doc was getting tired. We said goodbye, promising to see him again the next day. I was sad as we left the room, anxious for everyone to be well enough to leave. Doc's bullet wound had missed his spine but had hit a rib, bouncing over into his spleen before nicking something else. He'd be one organ short by the time he healed, but otherwise, he would fully recover.

When we rolled back into Jack's room, we came to an abrupt stop when we realized someone was in there. Daisy was standing with her back to the room as she stared out the window at the twinkling lights of Pumpkin Patch. I could see her whole body stiffen with our arrival.

I climbed off Jack's lap again, surprised when he didn't fight me that time. I walked over to Daisy and stepped beside her, seeing the town lit up below.

"Thank you, Daisy," I said softly. "What you did can never be repaid."

She inhaled sharply, then let it out in a whoosh. "I wish I could have done more. If I'd known who the other mole was…"

"Kara played her part well. Too well. I was certainly fooled." I shook my head in disgust at who I thought was my friend but who instead walked me right over to the devil with a smile on her face. "All that matters is that we all made it out alive. I'm sorry for killing your brother."

Daisy shrugged. "He was a shitty brother."

I tried to stifle a laugh, but Daisy started giggling, making me lose control until I was doubled over, clutching my side with tears leaking from the corners of my eyes. By the time we were done and brushing away the remnants of our laughter, Daisy was facing me with a smile.

"I'm really glad it's over."

I sighed as I looked over toward the bed where Jack was lying hooked back up to the machines and looking grumpy about it. "So am I. I just want to get back home and pretend none of this ever happened." I looked back at Daisy to see her swipe at her face. "You know you're welcome to stay."

She shook her head. "No. There's nothing here for me. I don't have any more family, and I burned too many bridges to stay. Besides, I found a nice place to land, and there is this guy I kinda like. I think I want to explore things with him and see if we have something special. Something like what you and Bones have."

I wrapped my arms around her shoulders and pulled her in for a big hug. Even after all the shit she had pulled and the hell she had put me through when we'd worked together, I knew, deep down, that she was a good person. Someone I would have liked to know.

"You'll stay in touch?" I asked as I stepped back.

She smiled, her lips trembling just a bit. "I'd like that."

I nodded. "Good."

She gestured toward the bed. "Do you mind if I say goodbye?"

I grinned at her. "I'd be pissed if you didn't."

I stayed by the window as Daisy slowly, but without hesitance, stepped over to Jack while he watched her approach. "Bones, I just wanted to let you know I'm leaving. I also wanted to say thank you for everything you have done for me. I wouldn't have survived if it wasn't for you. I didn't deserve your help, not before, and not at my brother's compound." She swiped at her eyes. "You're a good man, Bones."

She stepped back and gave me a small wave as she headed for the door, but paused when Jack called out to her.

"Stay safe. If you ever need anything, you let me know."

Daisy looked like she might cry but straightened her shoulders and firmed her lips as she acknowledged his words with a quick nod. Then she was leaving through the door, letting it close softly behind her.

After kicking off my shoes, I climbed into the bed with Jack and let him tuck me into his side. Neither of us said a word as we lay there quietly. We were both eager to get home. The doctor had promised that he might be able to leave tomorrow as long as Jack took care of himself. That was a promise I intended to make sure happened.

JACK

I lay back on the bed, listening as Sally moved around the house. I fucking hated being restricted. What I hated even more was not being able to help out with the daily things that needed to be done around the house and club. With Doc and I both laid up while healing from our injuries, it had been up to Barrel, Shock, and Tech to run the club, while Sally insisted on taking care of the majority of my business work. I finally insisted that I would have no issues dealing with paperwork while sitting on my ass. She fought me at first, but once I convinced her that I would lose my fucking mind if I didn't have something to occupy it, she gave in, bringing the stack of papers from my desk at the club.

Zero jumped on the bed where I was reclining against the headboard, and I ruffled his fur while Sally walked through the bedroom after turning off all the lights in the rest of the house. She smiled sweetly as she walked through the room, pausing at my side to drop a kiss on my cheek before heading to the bathroom. I heard the shower turn on, and I'd had enough.

"Bed, Zero." He gave a low woof, but after licking my hand, he jumped from the bed. I watched as he circled three times and pawed at his pillow before laying down with a huff. I thought of Sally as she climbed under the spray, pictured her naked body, and groaned. This invalid shit was more than I could take.

I climbed off the bed and held back a wince as my ribs groaned in protest. I pulled the sweatpants down my legs and kicked them into the corner. It was still too hard to bend down to pick things off the floor. I would have to make it up to my little Queen later. Once I was fully healed, I would treat her like the queen she was, making sure she didn't have to lift a finger. I was damn lucky she looked after me and took care of all the things I couldn't while I was laid up.

I gingerly climbed back onto the bed and thought about what I was going to do tonight. What I was going to have *her* do. I may not be able to give her the dicking I wanted and what I knew she really craved from me, but I would make tonight enjoyable. It would only be a couple more weeks before I would be able to give her all of me. But there was no way I could wait that long.

I heard the shower turn off and closed my eyes as I pictured her wet body. The way the water would drip off her perky nipples that had grown darker with her pregnancy. I licked my lips as I thought about the way they felt in my mouth. I would have that tonight. I fisted my cock as I waited. It wouldn't be long before she was finished in the bathroom.

When she walked into the room wearing a small pair of sleep shorts that showed off her toned legs and the smallest, thinnest fucking tank top known to man, I growled with my hand squeezing my cock.

"Get over here."

She startled with her hand on the light switch.

"Go ahead and turn it off." The bedside lamp was on. It would give me plenty of light to see what I had missed in the last two weeks. With a blush that rose from the tops of her breasts to spread up her neck and onto her beautiful face, she hit the lights. The lamp cast a warm glow over the bed, guiding her straight to me.

"Take off your clothes and climb on my face."

She brought a hand to the front of her neck and rubbed absently as her thighs pressed together. "Jack, I don't think—"

"Little Queen, if you don't climb on my face right now, I am going to get out of this bed and bend you over it. Would you rather do all the work or take the chance I could hurt myself more?"

"That's coercion, Jack." Her tone may have been admonishing, but her sweet giggle told me she wasn't opposed.

"I don't give a fuck. It's been almost three weeks since I had your taste in my mouth. I'm dying without it. Seeing you walk around this house with your sexy tits swaying and your hot as fuck body teasing me has my cock ready to explode." I took my hand off my length so she could see how swollen I was for her. "See what you do to me, little Queen?" I rubbed my thumb over the precome that was leaking from the tip and almost groaned at the sensation. I couldn't resist another pump of my tight fist before letting go and reaching down to grip my balls. "I need you. Now."

She swallowed hard as she watched my hand move. She looked like she wanted to argue, but I could see the moment her resolve broke, and her hands went to her top. With one swift movement, she had it torn over her head and dropped to the floor. I groaned as my hand involuntarily squeezed.

Her shorts were next. I licked my lips as I saw her wet cunt exposed to me. I needed her in my mouth. No more waiting. I shifted on the bed until my back was flat. "Climb up here. I want your pussy in my mouth. I need you to ride my face, baby."

She walked over, her nipples hard points on her breasts, and goosebumps spread over her arms. She hesitated at the side of the bed. "You'll tell me if you hurt?" I grunted, wanting to grab her and yank her to me, but I knew it would make her stop, and my plans would be ruined.

"I swear I won't move. You can do all the work, and I will stay perfectly still. But, little Queen, if you don't get on my face right now, the punishment you have coming to you when I am better will be so much worse." My words were barely understandable even to my own ears as I growled.

"Okay, Jack." She put one knee on the bed and hesitated until I gripped her hips in frustration and pulled. She grabbed onto the head-board with both hands. It was her turn to glare as she stared down at me. Her pussy was so close, I could smell it, but she held herself back. "I know you're used to being in control, but if you move a single muscle other than your tongue, I will stop."

I grinned up at her. "You're cute when you're mad. It's like a spitting kitten."

She narrowed her eyes. "I'm not messing around, Jack. No moving, or we're done. Got it?"

"Yes, ma'am. Now, give me my pussy."

She sighed in exasperation but shifted up my body. I could feel the heat of her wet cunt as it moved up my abdomen and chest. My cock was so hard I was worried I would come the second her taste hit my tongue. That was alright; I knew I had more than enough to give her. I'd be hard again before I was done eating her.

She hovered over my face, and I could see how wet she was, the moisture glistening on her folds and inner thighs.

"Sit!" I commanded. I had to grip the sheets at my sides to stop myself from grabbing her again. I knew my fierce little kitten would carry out her threat of stopping. She had grown so much since I had first seen her. She'd evolved from a scared little girl hiding behind her hair to the warrior queen who stared down two different evil men and won. I loved her so much more with every day that passed. I never knew it was possible to care about someone the way I did her. For so many years, I had just moved through life with a cold, dead heart. She brought me to life with one look of her beautiful blue eyes.

Gingerly, she lowered her pussy until it hovered just above my mouth. "Oh my god, this is so awkward," she mumbled. I stuck my tongue out and swiped through her wetness, my eyes nearly rolling in the back of my head.

"Don't think, just feel."

When my tongue glanced over her clit, she quivered, her knees lowering her a little more. When I slid my tongue through her wetness to swirl around her entrance, she trembled, gripping the headboard tight. When I sucked on her clit, she lost her battle with the grip on the bed and sank the rest of the way, nearly suffocating me. I groaned. I would die a happy man.

She gasped and rubbed frantically as I chuckled. Suddenly, her shyness and reservations were gone, and I was just the tool to be used to get her off. I had to grip my hard cock firmly at the base, hard, to stop myself from coming all over my stomach and her ass.

Within minutes, she was throwing her head back and screaming her pleasure to the ceiling. I wanted nothing more than to grab her, turn her onto her back, and pound my hard cock into her until I released every bit of my hot come into her depths. Instead, all I could do was pant as if I'd run a fucking marathon and hope that she would take pity on my aching balls.

She scooted back until her wet pussy rested on my abs, my hard cock trapped and throbbing as she rested her face in my neck. Her hot breath coated my skin as I squeezed my eyes shut and gritted my teeth. She had given me what I asked for. I wouldn't beg her to drop her cunt down on my cock and ride me into oblivion.

I kept my eyes closed and continued to pant when she lifted her head and shifted. I felt her pussy lips slide over my cock head and had to bite my tongue to keep in my groan. It was when she angled her hips to glide up and then back down to notch the head of my dick at her entrance that I finally opened my eyes.

Her voice was husky when she whispered down to me. "You're going to be a good boy and stay perfectly still."

I growled at her words, every part of me wanting to retake control, but I didn't dare move a muscle. I nearly whimpered when she glided down until I bottomed out inside of her.

"Fuck. Fuck, yes!" I finally broke, throwing back my head and shouting. It was a fight to stop from coming as her hot walls gripped me as tight as a fist. Soon, she was raising and lowering herself as she leaned back, balancing her hands on my thighs as her hair tickled my balls. I made the mistake of looking at where we were joined. Seeing my length glisten with her wetness in the lamplight as she slid up and down was more than I could take. With a primal grunt I felt deep in my chest, I was unloading every drop of come I had into her.

When my mind finally started working again, it was to see Sally leaning over me, her hands resting on the bed next to my head. She had a wicked grin on her face, and seeing her like that, I fell in love with her all over again. I would never stop falling for her.

"You were such a good boy," she cooed.

As I growled and snapped my teeth at her throat, she giggled before moving off my softening cock and curled up against my side. I moved my good arm around her shoulders, pulling her closer to me.

"I love you, little Queen."

"I love you, too, Jack Ellington."

Epilogue ~ Four Months Later

SALLY

Even though it's spring, and it still gets pretty freaking cold at night in April, the world around us had finally thawed out. To celebrate, bikers did it in the only way they knew how - with booze and fighting. And fucking, too, I was sure. Though I doubted they ever let a little ice and snow stop them from having a woman.

Jack helped me down from his big black truck, his hands sliding around to rest on my belly for a few extra long seconds as he felt his son kick against his hands with a grin. Jack rarely hid his smiles anymore. He was still the deadly cold President of the Devil's Night-mares, but he no longer felt the need to suppress his emotions. At least when it came to his little family.

The truck was the only vehicle in The Warehouse parking lot that wasn't on two wheels, but I thought it was pretty sweet of all the clubs to leave a spot just for us at the front of the building. I wasn't *that* big, though Jack's giant baby did leave me feeling like a beached whale most of the time. And to think I still had two more months to go. The obstetrician had already informed us that I would have to have a C-section due to the size of the baby. Jack had been pretty upset, but I just told him it was only one more scar. It was one that I would wear with pride.

Jack took my hand and led me over the dirt and gravel, carefully watching my every step to make sure I wouldn't slip, trip, or fall. It had been the same way for the last few months, and as much as I loved his overprotectiveness most of the time, sometimes I just wanted to pretend that I wasn't pregnant so he'd be rough with me again.

The doors were propped open just like they had been the last time I'd been here. It seemed like a lifetime ago when I entered this massive building for the first time. Back then, I'd been a scared little mouse, afraid of the noise and all the men that filled the place. I had wanted to hide myself from everyone, even if it had been impossible in those skimpy clothes the servers have to wear. There would be no shorts riding up my ass and tight crop tops showing far too much cleavage for me tonight. Instead, I was wearing what I hoped was a cute dress with a cardigan. I knew I was going to look ridiculous walking into a biker venue wearing a sundress, but there were only so many things I could wear these days that didn't include giant sweatpants and one of Jack's T-shirts.

As we walked inside, we were greeted by so many people I couldn't keep track. I did know that the President of the Black Wolves tried to touch my belly but backed off with a grin when Jack withdrew his knife from his belt. Luckily, he hadn't pulled the same move with all the club girls who cooed over my baby bump.

It took a while to reach Jack's designated table, which was already occupied by Doc. Shock and Barrel wandered over a few minutes later to shake hands as well as give Jack a hard time about driving a cage to fight night. Jack took their teasing good naturedly, though, flipping them off with a grin.

I snuggled into his side as the first round of drinks was brought to our table by one of the girls. I thanked Mindy and slipped her a nice tip for her trouble as she winked then walked away. We all turned when the announcer started speaking from the center of the huge ring in the middle of the concrete floor.

"Who's ready for fight night?"

Cheers went up through the building at the commencement of the

first fight night of the year. The announcer looked extremely disappointed as he shook his head, playing it up for all the bikers.

"I *said,* who's ready for mother fucking FIGHT NIGHT?"

The yells, stomping, and banging on the tables were so loud I had
to cover my ears while I laughed. The excitement was infectious, and
my heart started pounding with anticipation.

The first couple of guys were called into the ring. They were young
and were obviously new. I figured they were likely newly patched
members trying to prove something to their clubs. I gasped when the
first fight ended with the two on the ground. The one on top was
pounding the one trapped on the mat so hard that blood flew, adding
to the many stains that already covered the surface. As disturbing as it
was, I couldn't look away.

The fights continued the same way. Most of the fighters seemed to
be evenly matched, but sometimes, someone would go in and get
knocked out in the first few seconds. The poor guy was heckled so
badly I felt bad for him. But when his club brothers would retrieve the
loser, it was always with good natured pats on the back and a little bit
of ribbing thrown in. They never left too upset, though.

Then the moment came I had been anticipating with equal parts
excitement and dread. Jack's name was called, and just like months
ago, the whole room went wild. A flash of fear filled me for a moment
when I thought of his broken ribs and bullet wound, but I forced
myself to relax. The doctor had cleared him months ago. Since then,
Jack has been lifting weights and running in an effort to get his
strength and stamina back. I had been thrilled to see him able to work
out again because he was the biggest fucking baby on the planet while
injured.

Jack stood up from his seat and turned to look at me, a small smirk
playing on the corner of his lips. I licked my lips as he began to take
his leather cut off. He had never replaced it. There was still a bullet
hole above his name and title, which made it look pretty badass if I
were being honest. But the blood stains made me shiver every time I
looked at them. He folded it carefully and handed it to me, which I
took and immediately hugged to my chest.

The other guy he was set to fight was already in the ring, doing his best to get the crowd to back him. I wasn't certain it was working the way he'd hoped, though. Jack pulled off his shirt from over his head, making me squeeze my thighs together at the sight. I would never get over how handsome he was. The stark black of his tattooed body just added a wild, untouchable effect to the whole package that was him. Well, untouchable to everyone but me. He welcomed my touch anytime I wanted to run my hands over him. Which I seriously was tempted to do right at that moment while his arms flexed as he handed me his shirt.

He leaned down, placing his hand on my throat with gentle pressure. "I'll be right back, little Queen.

"Okay, Jack," I whispered against his lips right before he placed a hot kiss on my mouth. As he straightened up and began to walk away, I licked his taste that still lingered on my lips.

"Jesus, don't you two ever take a break?""

I flipped Barrel off without taking my eyes off Jack and listened to him roar in laughter. Jack gripped the side of the ring and vaulted himself up onto the edge with a nimble jump. He turned back to me with a wink before turning back around to step over the top rope.

His opponent stuck his finger out, pointing at Jack, and said something, probably taunting and stupid, but Jack just twisted his neck side to side, loosening up. As soon as the bell rang, the other biker ran full force at Jack. I shook my head in disgust. Didn't they ever learn? Jack took a step to the side just as the man reached him with his fist out, ready to swing. As he flew past, Jack kicked out his foot and shoved the guy in the ass, making him stumble forward into the ropes.

As everyone erupted in laughter, the guy turned around, his face beet red from embarrassment. Jack said something to him and then gestured in a come hither motion with two fingers at the biker. I cringed while unable to hold in my laughter.

From there, the fight continued, with Jack evading punches while getting hits in every time. The other guy was covered in blood from his leaking nose, and the last punch he'd received had him holding his back. Even from where I was sitting, I could see his face twisted in pain.

"That guy's gonna be pissing blood for a few days," Doc mumbled, then took a swig of his beer. It made me glad that Jack was as good as he was. I would have hated to see him hurt again.

Finally, it seemed like Jack was done playing cat and mouse and descended on the other biker. With a few swift punches to the gut and then one hard uppercut to the chin, the fight was over. The guy was lying on his back, breathing heavily, when Jack strolled over to him and bent down. I didn't know what he said to him, but the other man laughed and held out his hand. Jack gripped it tightly and then hauled the man to his feet. With a final shake of hands, Jack turned back to me.

Like last time, he ignored the crowd as he jumped down from the ring. He didn't even acknowledge anyone as they tried to congratulate him. Instead, his eyes were on me as he strode forward with long strides.

The look on his face was like a hungry panther. I swallowed hard as I stood up from the bench and waited. By the time he reached me, I was already panting, my panties damp, and my heart racing. I was eager for what I saw in his gaze.

His hand went straight to my neck as I raised my chin in offering. Without a word, he led me to the same back door we had had our first encounter. The hand that had slid from my throat to the back of my neck was tight with tension as we stepped outside. Nothing had changed from that first night. The tables were still arranged in the dirt, and there was still one single yellow bulb that barely lit up the yard.

There was no one outside this time as Jack kicked the door closed with one foot. He led me over to our table, and I started to sit.

"Not this time, little Queen," he rumbled in his deep, gravelly voice.

"Where do you want me, Bones?" I asked, hiding my grin.

He growled at me and then took my mouth in a rough kiss that I moaned into immediately. My Jack could be tender sometimes, but there was nothing I loved more than when he lost control and showed me his wild side. With firm hands, he gripped my hips and effortlessly lifted me to sit on top of the table.

With quick movements, he had the skirt of my dress flipped up, and my panties ripped down and off my legs. He bent over and licked up the center of my pussy. I leaned back on my elbows and moaned to the sky. I opened my eyes to stare at the stars filling the sky as he shoved my thighs wider to taste every part of me. When he wrapped his lips around my clit, the stars were behind my eyelids, flashing with brilliant lights as I screamed my release.

Before I could come back from nirvana, Jack had already undone his belt and had his pants open and shoved down his hips. He gripped my thighs hard enough to leave fingerprints as he pulled me to the edge of the table, careful not to make me collapse with his roughness, always mindful even through his raging lust. With one swift thrust, he was buried to the hilt inside me. Just like that, I was whole again.

I laid back fully on the table, needing to grip the wood above my head as he began to pound into me wildly. Every thrust sent a wave of euphoria through my entire being. Every glide of his hard cock hit just the right nerve ending to have me climbing higher and higher until I reached that pinnacle all over again.

Jack cursed and grunted above me as his cock grew impossibly thicker inside my channel. When his thrusts lost their rhythm, I was ready. Together, we broke apart, finding the bliss we had only ever found in each other. It would only be each other for us. There was no one else in the universe who could give us what each other could.

Epilogue ~ Two Years Later

THE NIGHTMARE KING

I rolled over and nuzzled into the back of my wife's neck. It was early morning; everything was quiet inside the house and in the world outside. No one was calling me, texting, or asking me questions. It was just me and my wife's sexy as fuck body cuddled against mine under our warm blankets.

"Ummm, Jack," she murmured sleepily without opening her eyes.

"Merry Christmas, baby. Go back to sleep," I said softly as my hand drifted up to cup her soft breast. Pregnancy and breastfeeding had given them more weight and size, and I was just enough of a horny man to admit they turned me the fuck on. I could hardly keep my hands, eyes, or dick off her gorgeous tits. When I titty fucked her several months ago while her milk rolled down to coat my cock, I thought I would lose my goddamn mind. I needed to get her pregnant again soon so I could experience that again.

I lifted her leg and placed it over my hip, widening her for my cock. I placed the tip of my cock at her entrance while she moaned into her pillow.

"Hurry up, Jack. Your son is going to be awake and ready to burn the world down soon." Her muffled words had me chuckling as I angled my hips and pressed forward as far as I could in our current positions.

Slow and steady, I rocked back and forth, giving my woman just enough of me to make her moan for more as she woke up fully. Once her moans changed to pleas for more, I rolled us until she was under me. I slid my arm under her hips and lifted, titling until she was at the perfect angle. Then I gripped her long braid, wrapping it around my fist.

With hard thrusts that would have put the headboard through the wall if I hadn't anchored it down more than a year ago, I gave Sally the Christmas morning wakeup call I had given her for the last two years and would continue to give until I was dead in the ground.

When she started to scream as her cunt began to spasm around my cock, I used my hold on her hair to muffle her cries with the pillow.

"Fuck. Fuck. Fuck. Always so fucking good, baby," I panted, doing my best to hold off my orgasm but knowing that it was a futile effort. Her heat, wetness, and tight stranglehold on my cock all worked against me, forcing me to come in several powerful spurts as I held my hips pressed as tight against her ass as I could get.

I rolled her back over onto her side, refusing to pull out of her, as we both panted for air. "You're going to kill me," she groaned as I felt an aftershock run through her body.

"Never," I growled back, nipping her chin with my teeth.

She giggled, slapping my face away weakly when the sound of our son suddenly drifted to us. Zero jumped to his feet and ran to the door. He sat there and cocked his head one way then the other as he listened to the increasingly loud demand came from down the hall.

"Da da da da da da da!"

"It's times like this that I'm glad he hasn't said mama yet."

I swatted Sally's ass before sliding out of her, wishing I had time to enjoy the sight of my come leaking from her body.

"Get your ass up and go pee," I demanded, even more determined than when we'd first started our relationship, that my little Queen take good care of herself. Sometimes, she grumbled about my insistence that she pee to prevent a UTI after sex, but she still did it, knowing that it was out of concern for her wellbeing and not a need to control her.

I slid out of bed and quickly pulled a pair of sweatpants on. As soon as I opened the door, Zero took off, running to the next door down the hall, pawing at it impatiently. I was pretty sure he loved my son more than me at this point. When I opened Timmy's door, Zero ran straight to the side of the crib and immediately began to bark and whine while Timothy giggled uproariously.

"Come on, little monster." I scooped my son up and held him close to my chest, taking in the feel of him against me and hating that he seemed to be growing faster than I could keep up. It seemed just a week ago he'd been so small I was afraid I would crush him if my hand spasmed. Sally swore that he had always been a giant baby, but holding him now, all I remembered was how tiny he was. It's too bad I couldn't turn back time and start it over again from the moment he was placed in my arms.

I scrunched up my nose as soon as the smell hit me. I looked over my shoulder to our bedroom, then down at Zero, who gave me a chastising "woof."

"Fine, I'll do it myself."

After cleaning up the mess of breakfast that somehow ended up on the ceiling, Sally and I began the long process of getting ready to take our eighteen-month-old out of the house. While Sally triple-checked the diaper bag, I pulled the truck up to the front of the house to get it warm and to keep the trip in the icy weather as short as possible for both my wife and son.

I closed the door behind me and rubbed my hands together to warm them up. "Looks like you're getting the white Christmas you hoped for."

Sally gasped and ran to the front door, jerking it open to stare in wonder at the white wonderland outside. "It's so pretty," she breathed.

I chuckled softly and wrapped my arm around her waist. No matter how often she saw the world covered in snow, she always reacted the same.

Zero gave a warning bark, and I bent down to scoop up my little monster before he could get past our legs and run out into the snow. The last time he had done that, he landed face-first in the cold wetness and cried for fifteen minutes straight.

"Come on, we have Christmas to celebrate." I nibbled on his neck, making his whines turn to giggles. I waited until Sally set the alarm and locked the front door as I held Timothy. Together, we walked to the idling truck as I scanned the ground for rocks or ice. I had the prospects keep all the walkways clear, but I still checked for myself every night, so it should be clear of hazards, but it was always best to be sure.

The ride to the clubhouse was short, as usual. As we drove slowly past the house that Doc built this last summer, I watched him and Helen step out onto their front porch. Sally waved frantically as if we hadn't just had dinner with them last night. Doc scowled at the ground and wrapped his arm around his wife's waist as he practically carried her to his SUV. He lifted her inside while she kept one hand on her huge belly and waved back as we passed.

As soon as I parked in my designated spot, the front door of the clubhouse flew open, and three children with various shades of red hair came running out.

"Sally! Sally! Come inside, quick! Santa came!"

"Mama said we had to wait for you to get here before we can open our presents," the youngest grumbled with their arms folded over their chest.

"Well, then, I guess we better get inside!" Sally told her siblings as they turned around and ran back the way they came.

Sally's parents only came around once a year, and while they were around, they mostly sat alone on the couch. They seemed happy to let their children run around while my brothers or club girls attempted to corral them. I always waved off Sally's apologies. I knew she felt bad about her family's behavior, but I was just glad they were communicating. It had been a rocky start when Sally made the first phone call to her parents. But after a few rough minutes, everyone calmed down, and her parents listened carefully to every word as Sally described what she had been through. Sally was happy to have them back in her life, even if it was mostly long distance. I was just glad I didn't have to murder my woman's parents.

I looked around the mess in the room, seeing piles of ripped paper and ribbons. There were torn boxes from where the kids had hastily removed toys from their packaging before quickly discarding them for the next present.

It was complete mayhem.

But as I glanced down at my wife tucked snugly under my arm and our son asleep against my chest with his new stuffed dinosaur held loosely in his arms, I realized I didn't care.

I had everything I could ever want in my arms.

Everyone I cared about was within these walls.

My woman looked up at me, sensing my stare. I leaned down and pressed a kiss to her lips. It had been a hard beginning. My mother-in-law once said that we were lucky our lives together ended the way they did. She thought we might not have made it through, that any little thing could have changed the outcome. The possibilities were endless. I could have died if Daisy hadn't grown a conscience. Sally may not have even come to Pumpkin Patch if her finger had landed an inch over. I could have been sitting in prison if I hadn't stopped myself from killing Dr. Stein in the hotel room.

But I refused to believe that. Sometimes, fate refused to be messed with, and the outcome would always end the same, regardless of the journey. That's what I believed as I looked into the gorgeous blue eyes of my wife as she mouthed the words that I had hoped to hear today. I squeezed her closer to my side as I grinned down at her and slid my hand over her belly, which was softer than it had been a couple of years ago before giving me our first child. Soon, our little family would grow larger. I hadn't known I was capable of loving someone the way I loved my little Queen, but it was written in the stars.

We were simply meant to be.

THE END

Acknowledgments

Thank you so much for reading! This was a fun story to write since it combined my love of NBC, creativity, and romance! I already know that it is impossible to do Jack and Sally justice, I just hope that I was able to somehow create an entertaining story that you could enjoy.

Thank you to my alpha/beta team: Christina, Lucy, and Brittany thank you for all the feedback! Feya and Melissa, your notes are invaluable! Finally, Nicole, I couldn't do this without you. Those aren't just words, ladies, they come from the depths of my heart.

As always, I welcome feedback. If there is something you find that needs correcting, I'd love to hear about. Please feel free to contact me at rsullinsauthor@gmail.com.
Please join my Facebook group for giveaways, and sneak peeks into what I might currently be working on.

RSullins Rogue Readers

If you enjoyed the story, please consider leaving a review! It truly is the best way to show an author that you care.

R. Sullins is a USA Today bestselling author, an International Bestseller, and a KDP All Star.

Family is number one in her life, followed by her menagerie of pets. Be patient with her, she's not very good at peopling.

She is a lover of fairies, tattoos, and coffee cups, has a vast collection of them all, and receives a glare from her teenager every time she brings home a new cup to squeeze into the cabinet.

When she's not writing, you will probably be able to find her reading a book. But, no matter what genre you find her immersed in, there is always one thing that her favorite stories have in common… you will never, ever find her reading any book with cheating. So rest assured! She will never write one, either.

A bit of drama, a dash of spice, a little bit of innocence, and a large dab of alpha is what makes up the recipe for her stories. Find more of her here: www.rsullins.com

She wasn't sure what she was doing at the cabin.

It was run down and needed serious attention.

She should sell it and be done with it, but her grandmother left it to her.

It was all she had left in the world.

He hadn't shifted back into his human form for years.

He held the responsibility for his family's death in his heart.

The only thing that kept him moving one paw in front of the other

was the need to make sure the same fate didn't happen to anyone else in his pack.

Then everything changed when a new scent filled the forest.

How was the Alpha wolf supposed to stay away when her scent just kept drawing him in?

TEMPTING THE WOLF BY R SULLINS